# The Essence of the Thing

# The Essence of the Thing

a novel

## Madeleine St John

CARROLL & GRAF PUBLISHERS, INC.
NEW YORK

First published in England by Fourth Estate Limited

First Carroll & Graf edition 1998

Carroll & Graf Publishers, Inc.
19 West 21st Street
New York, NY 10010-6805

Library of Congress Cataloging-in-Publication Data is available.
ISBN:0-7867-0560-4

Manufactured in the United States of America

*For Judith McCue*

# I

Nicola was still standing in the doorway when Jonathan began to speak: she hadn't had time even to take off her coat. It was a cold spring evening: one still needed a coat out of doors after dark.

She was standing there in the sitting-room doorway, her hands in her pockets, holding on to the packet of cigarettes she had gone out to buy, and the loose change, and the keys; she hadn't had time even to put these things on the table, and take off her coat, and sit down, because Jonathan had called out to her as soon as she'd shut the front door behind her. 'Nicola?' But in a tone of voice which seemed odd to her: too sharp, too urgent: and she'd stood, perplexed, in the doorway, her fingers having suddenly tightened around the cigarettes, the keys, the loose coins: 'What is it?' she said. *Is something wrong?*

Jonathan was sitting at the far end of the sofa; he turned his head just enough to enable his eye to catch hers. He gazed at her for a moment and then he spoke again. 'Come in here,' he said. 'I want to talk to you.'

What was he saying? Nicola was paralysed by dread – a dread which in weaker doses had become almost familiar to her during the past few months: now, with this preposterous invitation, *Come in here* (for where else might she have gone?), this ominous announcement, *I want to talk to you*, she saw that something wholly dreadful had at last begun. She saw this, but part of her mind failed truly to grasp it. So she stood, dumbfounded, in the doorway. 'What is it?' she asked again. 'What's wrong?'

*Wrong* is one of those words which sound like what they signify, not by virtue of onomatopoeia, but by virtue of a more subtle correspondence: the same being true, to a lesser degree only, of *right*. There is *right* and there is *wrong*: the knowledge that there is right and wrong is part of one's English-speaking birthright: these attributes could not imaginably achieve the same terrible finality in another formulation. This is right, said the Anglo-Saxon warrior, *and that is wrong*. And to be in the wrong is to be cast into a waste of ice and darkness which is the *ultima Thule* of devastation. One might nevermore return. 'Is anything wrong?' She could see as she uttered the word that something was, indeed, *wrong*. The ice and darkness filled the room.

Jonathan shrugged very slightly and then got impatiently to his feet. He leaned an arm against the mantelpiece; if there had been a fire he would certainly have poked it. As it was, he looked unseeingly at the objects at his elbow and moved a china poodle dog. Then he looked up at her again. 'There's no nice way to say this,' he said. 'But I've decided – that is, I've come to the *conclusion* – that we should part.' The ice and darkness were now inside her: all her entrails froze.

'I think I'll sit down,' she said. Her entrails had frozen, but her ankles had turned to water. She walked unsteadily over to the sofa and sat down, huddling her coat closer around her. Her hands were still in the pockets, still holding on to the cigarettes, and the loose change, and the keys. She dared not look at him, and yet she knew she must. She saw that Jonathan's face was a perfectly composed mask of calm assurance.

There was still a part of Nicola's mind which did not believe that this conversation was really taking place, and so it was possible to enter further into it. It was a sort of joke, it was the sort of joke which might be perpetrated in a dream: in the alternative reality where there was no right, no wrong. There's nothing wrong, she found herself thinking: this is just a sort of joke which I haven't yet understood. 'I don't think I understand,' she said. 'Could you just say all that again?'

# 2

Jonathan had been looking downwards, as if in search of the atavistic poker, the atavistic fire; he now looked up once more. 'I want you to move out,' he said. 'Sorry – there really isn't a nice way to say this, as I said before. Sorry. It just isn't working. I mean, you must know that as well as I do.'

'Move out,' Nicola repeated dazedly. There was this dreadful lurching feeling in her stomach and she had begun to tremble. Her fingers closed more tightly around the keys, the money, the cigarettes. This was a very nasty kind of joke; it did not seem possible that it could ever become funny.

'Yes,' said Jonathan. 'Well – that is – I've thought about this, obviously—' He was suddenly on much firmer ground: he was down to brass tacks, now. Brass tacks were his stock-in-trade, he being after all a lawyer. 'I mean, yes, *I* could move out, of course, and you could stay here, if you wanted to, but I just assumed you wouldn't want to take it on. I mean, I'm offering, obviously, to buy you out.'

Her state of shock was only intensified by each succeeding sentence. He was offering – obviously! – to buy her out. She had said nothing, and so he went on. He was looking carefully at the china poodle dog. 'I'm assuming, of course, that you wouldn't want to buy *me* out.'

Couldn't. He means, *couldn't*. How very tactful. Of course she *couldn't*. Nicola worked in the publications department of a famous, but medium-sized, arts organisation. She found that she was not trembling quite so much now, and might dare to speak.

'No,' she said, quite evenly. 'I wouldn't.' There was a very brief pause: you could hear the silence. 'In fact,' she went on, 'I wouldn't want you to buy me out *either*. In fact, Jonathan, I don't believe I know what you're talking about. I don't believe this conversation is really happening.' She got up. 'Look, I'm going to hang up my coat,' she said. 'And I'm going to make some tea, okay? And then you can tell me all about it. Because just at this precise moment I don't understand what the fuck you're on about. Excuse me.' And she left the room.

# 3

And although she was still in a state of extreme shock, and still trembling, she was beginning now to see – to realise – *to understand* – that the thing which was truly wrong was not so much the dreadful scene into which she had just been precipitated, as the misapprehension (whatever it might be) which had given rise to it: she was beginning now to understand – and she became more certain by the minute – that Jonathan's 'conclusion', however rational in itself, could have derived only from a hugely wrong, a wholly false, initial assumption, and that all that was now necessary was the careful discovery of this assumption and the calm revelation of its falseness. Now that she knew what she must do there was nothing truly to worry about, nothing truly to fear. She had stopped trembling; she went and made the tea, and took it into the sitting room.

They were both silent while she poured it out; she handed Jonathan – still standing at the mantelpiece – a cup and then she began to take the cellophane off the cigarette packet.

'I've asked Winkworth's to send someone round on Monday morning to do a valuation,' Jonathan said. 'I thought that was the fairest way. Property prices haven't moved much since we bought this place, but I thought if we got a valuation now, I'd be prepared to give you your share of the current value *or* your original stake, whichever is the greater. If you see what I mean. Can't say fairer than that; I hope you agree.'

Nicola lit a cigarette. 'Yes,' she said. 'Couldn't possibly be fairer.'

She inhaled. 'There is a problem, though,' she went on. 'Oh, I suppose you're thinking about the f and f,' said Jonathan. 'I'm sure we can sort that out easily enough.' 'No, that's not it,' said Nicola.

'What then?'

'Jonathan, do sit down.' He looked reluctant, but did so. She took another drag. Even though she had seen what she must do, it wasn't easy to begin. 'The problem,' she said, '*the* problem is, that I don't actually understand what all this is about. I mean, something has evidently gone wrong, badly wrong: and I don't have a clue what it is.'

Jonathan looked surprised, and even slightly pained. 'No,' he said. 'Nothing's *gone wrong*. Nothing in particular, that is. No, truly. It's just the whole thing. It's us. *We're* wrong. I mean, as a couple. I thought you'd realised that as well as I had. You know how it's been. Well. Need I go into it?'

If this was the initial assumption, the revelation of the falseness of which would lead to the collapse of Jonathan's entire argument, then hard as it had been to begin, it would be harder still to continue: his speech had thrown her into a state of even deeper shock and pain. She began to tremble again.

'I evidently don't know *how it's been*,' she said shakily. 'Of course we've had out sticky moments, every couple does, but – but – *I* thought we were happy.' And with these words she began, at last, to cry. Her tears began to fall quite heavily; she could not speak further, and began even to sob. Jonathan, sitting at the other end of the sofa, took a handkerchief from his pocket and handed it to her silently – a large square of rumpled, but clean, linen. She buried her face in it and wept uncontrollably for some minutes. The world she had inhabited having been smashed to pieces (whose jagged edges cut her wherever she turned), it was the only natural thing to do.

# 4

Jonathan waited, staring into the fire which was not there, until Nicola's tears subsided; at last she blew her nose, and looked up. She could almost have wished her tears to continue, for the icy darkness of this dreadful new consciousness. Whatever was wrong was deeper and more secret an affair than she could have guessed. It lay in the very heart of their lives, it lay in them, it lay, for all one knew, in their actual souls: if souls they possessed.

'I don't understand you,' she said once more. 'I don't understand anything you've said.' And she could not have spoken, could never have spoken, so truly. Her whole mind was black with incomprehension. Jonathan had stood up again; he leaned once more against the mantelpiece. 'I think that rather proves my point, doesn't it?' he said.

Even now she could not quite believe that he could say such a thing to her, at such a moment. She was silenced, but at the same time she found that tears had once more filled her eyes. She picked up the handkerchief and wiped them away, but more came; she was on the point of sobbing again. 'It's just the shock,' she found herself thinking; 'it's simply the shock.'

Jonathan made a shrug of impatience. '*Please* don't cry any more,' he said. 'It really isn't helpful.' He poured some more tea into her cup. 'Here, drink this,' he said. 'You'll feel better.'

She left the tea where it was. 'I'm sorry you've taken this so – hard,' he said. She knew, instantly, that he had been on the point of saying 'badly', and had stopped himself just in time. 'I really didn't expect it. That you should have thought we were *happy* was the last thing I expected. But there you are. We don't understand each other, as you said. We'll be much better off by ourselves.' And he said this almost with satisfaction. It was clear that he thoroughly believed it.

It was only now that the likeliest, the most banal, explanation occurred to Nicola's dazed and grief-stricken mind.

'Is there someone else?' she said. She looked at his face carefully, steadily. His surprise was unmistakable; he even looked rather affronted by the suggestion. 'No, of course not,' he said. 'I would have told you if there had been.'

There was a pause. 'No,' he continued. 'No one else. Just *us*.' 'Us,' she repeated. 'And now, it seems, there's no *us*.' He said nothing: an infinite boredom seemed to have possessed him: she recognised that expression, she remembered this sensation: he had hardened his heart, and closed his mind, against her. He would answer no questions, he would be cold to every appeal; she was altogether, for the present time at least, shunned. She recognised that expression, she remembered this sensation of death-in-life, and she was filled with a desolation which made her tears of a few minutes ago seem luxurious. 'Jonathan,' she said; 'don't *do* this.'

He ignored her. She might not have spoken. He picked up the tea-tray. 'I'll sleep in the spare room,' he said. 'Are there sheets in there?' She looked away from him with a kind of disgust, and ignoring this too he went on. 'And by the way, I'll be away at the weekend – parents.' Just so. And tomorrow was Friday. 'I'll go straight down after work. Okay?' She shrugged slightly, still speechless, and got up. 'Well, good night,' he said blandly. 'I'll see you in the morning.' She stared at him dumbly, and left the room. Having been cast out by him, she now found – as she had found before – that she was capable only of speaking and acting, even to a degree apparently of feeling, like a stranger.

But struggling, terrified and helpless, a loving and trusting Nicola shrieked in anguish from the depths of this stunned and frozen stranger.

# 5

'Are you doing anything tonight?'

'Not particularly.'

'Can I come round after work?'

'Just you?'

'Yes. Just me.'

'Is anything wrong?'

'Ish.'

'Oh?'

'I'll tell you when I see you.'

'I'm afraid Geoff'll be here. It's one of his days off.'

'It doesn't matter. Look, I'll bring something to drink. Is there anything else you'd like?'

'No, something to drink will do nicely.'

'I'll see you later then, around six-thirty, okay?'

'Yes, see you then. Take care.'

'You too.'

Susannah hung up.

'Who was that?'

'Nicola.'

'What does she want?'

'Me.'

'Why?'

'A friend in need.'

'Oh? Something wrong?'

'She says ish. I dare say we'll find out tonight.'

'Oh, God. She's not going to go on and on, is she? I might go out and leave you girls to it.'

'As you like. We can manage without you.'

'Is she coming here for supper?'

'Well, naturally. She's coming straight from work. She's bringing something to drink.'

'Tell you what. I'll stay until we've eaten and then I'll bugger off down the pub.'

'It's karaoke night.'

'All the better.'

'I thought you liked Nicola.'

'She's a sweetheart.'

'So?'

'I just don't like women going on and on.'

'Exactly what do you mean by that?'

'You know. On and on. Complaining. Usually about a man.'

'If only there were never any occasion to.'

'Come, now. You don't hear us men going on and on.'

'You have no occasion to.'

'Can it really be as simple as that?'

'Possibly not. Well, that's interesting, isn't it. The thing that's wrong with women is that they go on and on, and the thing that's wrong with men is that they don't.'

'Do you think I should do my Joe Cocker number tonight, or that Bryan Ferry one?'

'Honestly, Geoff. This is no time for joking. Nicola might be in real *trouble*.'

'Not her. That chic little Nothing Hill set-up with the deluxe plumbing and the stuffed shirt laying down the old claret. No way. She probably just wants some help with her vol-au-vents.'

'Geoffrey: you are *an idiot*. I think you'd really better make yourself scarce tonight after all. Do the Joe Cocker. Now bugger off and let me get some work done.'

Susannah worked from home, and Geoffrey was a lecturer at a former polytechnic, so between them they just managed to service the mortgage on a house in Clapham which they had bought before the neighbourhood became quasi-fashionable. They had one clever child; they could not afford another. Later on that day Susannah gave Geoffrey a shopping list and he went to Sainsbury's and got everything in, plus some caramels.

'What's this?' said Susannah, unpacking.

'Caramels.'

'What for?'

'For you.'

'*Me?*'

'Yes, why not?'

'*Why?*'

'A token of my esteem.'

'Oh, I wish.'

'And my love, admiration, gratitude, etcetera.'

'Oh, yeah. Want one?'

'Well, since you ask. Just one.'

The clever child, a boy of nine, at this moment came home from school. 'Cor!' he said. 'You're eating *sweets*! Cor!'

'Well, we've been good today,' said his father.

'So what else is new?' said the child, whose name was Guy.

'Give me a kiss,' said his mother. 'Alright,' said Guy, and obliged. 'Want one?' she asked, offering the caramels. He took one. 'Do you want to see my poem?' he asked them. He was invited to read it to them, and did so. 'Cor!' said Susannah. 'That's really whizzy. Well done!' 'I wish I could write like that,' said Geoffrey. He meant it, too: any adult might have wished as much. But there you were.

# 6

They were all sitting around the kitchen table eating spaghetti and drinking the wine Nicola had brought, except for Guy, who was drinking chocolate-flavoured milk. When they were all done, Guy obtained permission to go and watch television and the adults sat back and sighed at each other.

'So how's Jonathan?' said Susannah.

Nicola was smoking a cigarette. She fiddled with her lighter. 'I'm not exactly sure,' she said. 'Are there grounds for concern?' asked Susannah, who had from the inception of this relationship believed that there just possibly could be.

'Well. You see . . .'

'Go on.'

'I went out last night to buy some cigarettes.'

'Oh, yes?'

'We'd been sitting around watching telly; it was a perfectly average evening.'

'Yes, I know the sort of thing you mean, we have those too.'

'And so, anyway, I went out to the pub and got the fags and came straight back, and when I got in, Jonathan called out to me and said, Come in here, I want to talk to you. So I did, I mean I hadn't even had a chance to take off my coat, and he told me, he said—'

She broke off.

'Yes?'

'He said, I want you to move out.'

'He *what?*' cried Susannah.

'Just like that?' asked Geoffrey.

'Yes, just like that.'

Her interlocutors sat there, stunned and appalled.

'I mean,' said Susannah, 'had you no suspicion beforehand—'

'No, none. I mean, absolutely *none.*'

'He must be round the twist.'

'He seemed perfectly rational.'

'That's when they're at their worst.'

'Ho hum,' said Geoffrey.

'You shut up, you,' said Susannah.

He ignored this. 'What happened then?' he asked.

'Well—' said Nicola; and at some length she managed to relate the rest of the conversation and to describe the sensations which it had induced in her.

Her friends were still appalled but they were no longer stunned.

'He's a complete and utter rat,' said Susannah. 'It's a merciful release.'

'Do you really think so?' said Nicola unhappily. The relating of the tale had left her shaken.

'Absolutely,' said Susannah. 'He's *a rat.*'

'Well, perhaps not exactly a rat,' said Geoffrey. 'But certainly a prat. A prat, definitely. But that was always obvious. I mean, just look at the guy. You're better off without him, *much.*'

'But I love him,' said Nicola, and burst into tears. Susannah slid her chair around until it was beside Nicola's, and put her arm around her friend's shaking shoulders. 'There, have a good cry, darling,' she said. 'Susannah's here.' She continued to hold her as close as she could, patting her back from time to time, and meanwhile she turned her head and shot a withering look at her husband. '*Piss off,*' she mouthed at him, and after raising his eyebrows he muttered an excuse and got up and left the room.

'There,' said Susannah, 'there, there. Have a good cry. Stupid men. There, there.'

# 7

Nicola at last dried her tears, and sat silent and desolate while Susannah made some tea. She looked down at her teacup. 'Jonathan may be a rat,' she said. 'That is, he is acting like a rat, at the moment. And he might go on being a rat now for good. But he isn't a prat. Truly he isn't. I know you think so, but really he isn't.'

'That was Geoff's word, not mine,' said Susannah.

'But I suppose you agree,' said Nicola.

'Well, every rat is *ipso facto* a prat,' Susannah pointed out.

Nicola had on reflection to concur. 'Alright then,' she said. 'Let's say he's a prat. But he's the prat I love.' She paused. 'Actually, I've never been absolutely sure what *prat* means, exactly.'

'I've never been absolutely sure what *love* means, exactly.'

'It means, that even when someone acts like a rat, and/or a prat, you still want to stay with them.'

'Some people would call that masochism.'

'Oh.'

The abyss opened up before her. Who knew what anything meant, exactly? How far into that darkness would one have to fall, or painstakingly climb, before one discovered meaning and truth – even assuming that they were, ultimately, there to be found? She scrambled as far away from the edge as she presently could.

'The trouble is,' she said, 'that one goes on fancying a person. No matter how badly they might behave.'

'Yes, that is the trouble, alright,' said Susannah. 'That's all the trouble.'

'It must be a sort of trick,' said Nicola, wondering. 'To make sure that we go on reproducing, no matter what. Not that sex these days has anything to do with reproduction; but still.'

'We're hooked up to the old mechanism, nevertheless. It's a mean old trick alright.'

They were both silent for a while. Susannah at last very tentatively spoke. 'Did this thing last night,' she said, 'really come out of the blue? Had you really no idea that it might be in his mind?'

Nicola didn't answer immediately She was trying to collect her memories and her thoughts. 'There have been a few rat-like moments,' she said. 'But nothing like this. Nothing suggesting this.' She paused again, and sat, thinking. 'Perhaps I've been simply obtuse,' she said slowly.

'I always think it's better to be obtuse than paranoid,' said Susannah.

Nicola smiled wanly. 'At least the paranoid are always prepared,' she said. 'For the worst, I mean.'

'Were you prepared for the best?' asked her friend. There, at last, clearly, it was. 'Yes,' said Nicola. 'I thought it was only a matter of time, I mean, not very much time, before we'd decide to marry.'

'Marriage being "the best", eh?'

'It must be, mustn't it?'

'Until we think of something even better.'

'What could that be?'

'Ah, if we only knew.'

Guy entered the room. 'Tell us,' said Susannah, 'what could be better than marriage, Guy?' 'Salvation,' he replied. His elders howled. 'Where do you learn these words?' asked Susannah. 'I learned that in RE,' said Guy. 'I'm not sure exactly what it means, but it's meant to be very good, so it might be better than marriage.'

'Can't you have both?'

'Well, I suppose so, but salvation is still probably the better of the two.'

'The better of the two,' repeated Susannah. 'Very good, Guy. Very good.' 'OK,' he said. He now remembered what he had come in for. 'Can I have another caramel?'

# 8

'What's your dad doing?'

'Watching telly.'

'Take him a caramel then.'

The child departed and the two women sat looking at each other for a moment. 'Lucky you,' Nicola sighed. 'Your turn will come,' said Susannah.

'Do you really think so?'

'Yes, of course I do. As soon as you get free of that rat.'

Nicola's face was a portrait of misery. She did not want to be free of Jonathan; her present situation was so intolerable that it could not truly be pondered, or even admitted: even here, now, with Susannah, she could look only at its edges, not at the excruciating whole.

'Jonathan isn't a rat *really*,' she said, almost wildly. 'He isn't— it's just—something's gone *wrong* somewhere. I mean, it's probably my fault. I just haven't had a chance to *talk* to him properly. I don't know what's in his mind. It must be my fault: I must have done something wrong.'

'He should have told you what it was, then, when you did it, not waited, and then—this.'

'Yes, well, it's difficult for him—he's—you know—perhaps he was too shocked, or confused—I don't know.'

She broke off, near to tears again. 'Listen, darling,' said Susannah, 'he may or may not be a fully paid-up rat but he's landed you in it good and proper, causing grief to you and consternation to your friends. As far as I'm concerned, if he doesn't shape up and talk this through to your mutual satisfaction as soon as he gets back from his cowardly weekend away, then the thing for you to do is to eff off out of the place *immédiatement* and leave him to it. Just pack a bag and *go*. I don't know what your alternatives may be but you know you're entirely welcome to come and crash here until you get sorted. But I mean, no pissing about. Either he shapes up and explains himself and makes a most profound apology and a guarantee of no further similar scenes – that is, if you really *do* want as you say to stay with him – *or* you get the fuck out of his rat-like way. You can sleep in my workroom. I'll even clear some space for your things. I can't say fairer than that.'

'You're an angel,' said Nicola miserably. 'But I can only hope that I won't need to take advantage of your generosity.'

'Never mind that: just promise me that you won't hang about. I mean it. I know rats. If there's one thing they love to do, it's prolong the agony. Do you promise? You'll telephone me on Monday evening, alright, at the latest Tuesday, *either* to assure me that the situation's sorted out, *or* to say that you're on the way here: is that understood?'

'You're an angel.'

'Yes,' said Susannah, 'that's me, definitely.'

# 9

Nicola had gone home in a taxi, Guy had gone to bed, Susannah was washing up and Geoffrey was hovering in her vicinity, giving an impression of helpfulness.

'What's she going to do, then?' he said.

'I don't know. It's too soon to decide.'

'Too *soon*?' How long does it take? He's told her to push off, it doesn't seem to me that there's anything to hang about for.'

'Ah, little do you know.'

'So tell me.'

'Well, doesn't it occur to you that he's obviously had a rush of blood to the head, or something of the kind? I mean, to suddenly come along and give an order like that, for no evident reason – well, it's perfectly mad.'

'Oh – so you think this is just a fit of temporary insanity. Total withdrawal of affection while the balance of his mind was disturbed.'

'Well, it might be. Something like that, anyway. I mean, it was so awfully sudden, so unforseen—'

'We have only Nicola's word for that.'

'Well, one has to trust her version in the absence of any others.'

'Alright, for the sake of the argument, it's totally sudden and unforeseen and therefore possibly irrational. But who wants to go on living with a bloke who can behave like that?'

'Nicola does.'

'Then she must be mad too. They're a dangerous pair.'

'Then they're best off staying with each other. Like the Carlyles.'

'She never struck me as mad before.'

'As a matter of fact, she isn't. I wouldn't have said what I did, but it was just one of those irresistible debating points.'

'No, I think you must be right. If she wants to stay with him, she must be mad.'

'No, she is *not mad*.'

'What then?'

'She *loves* him.'

'Oh, God, spare me.'

'What, *spare* you? Why?'

'*Love*. For God's sake. What does it *mean*?'

'You tell me. I seem to remember being presented with a whole bag of caramels, for my very own, this very afternoon, in token of your *love* for *me*, among other things.'

'Well, that's completely different.'

'How?'

'The way I feel about you couldn't possibly be compared to the way Nicola feels about Jonathan.'

'Why ever not?'

'Well, for God's sake. You're being disingenuous, aren't you?'

'No, truly not. I genuinely want to know what you mean.'

'Our situation is totally different from theirs. They couldn't either of them possibly feel as do either of us. Their situation is completely different, and so are they. Nothing is comparable.'

'That doesn't mean she can't love him, in her way, according to her nature and her situation.'

'Alright, but I can't take that kind of love seriously.'

'I think that's very intolerant of you, not to say arrogant, to say nothing of unimaginative.'

'Yes, that sounds like me.'

'So what could you possibly know about love?'

'Do you have to be tolerant, and humble, and imaginative, to know anything about love?'

'Yes.'

There was a moment's silence, and then Geoffrey spoke. 'I think,' he said slowly, 'you've just made a serious point. How disconcerting.'

'Well, we were having a serious conversation, weren't we?'

'Were we?'

'For heaven's sake. We were talking about love. After all.'

'And nothing is more serious than love.'

'No, nothing. Nothing, nothing, nothing.'

There was another brief silence. 'Actually,' said Geoffrey reflectively, 'I suppose nothing is *as* serious as love.'

'No, nothing. Nothing whatsoever.'

'Love, eh?'

'Yeah. Love.'

'Listen. Don't ever tell anyone I said that, will you? About nothing being as serious as love. I'll never be able to show my face on a squash court again.'

'When did you ever show your face on a squash court?'

'Well, you know what I mean. It's the principle of the thing.'

'Alright. I mean, when all's said and done, what would I want with a man who had no squash court credibility?'

'*Exactly.*'

# 10

'All the same, I still can't see how a reasonably intelligent and actually attractive lady like Nicola—'

'Oh, you think she's intelligent do you?'

'Yes, and attractive, yes; how she can—'

'I didn't realise you thought she was attractive.'

'Well, isn't she?'

'Apparently.'

'Right. So I can't see how she could love a twit like Jonathan.'

'He's rather tasty.'

'*What?*'

'If you like that sort of thing.'

'You can't be serious.'

'Try me.'

'How?'

'That's your problem.'

'God. Jonathan. *Tasty.* God.'

'I think they make quite a good couple, in a way. They look right together.'

'*Look* right?'

'Yes, you know. They look good together.'

Geoffrey, still astounded, did his best to consider this proposition. 'I *suppose* they do,' he said. 'I *suppose* they do.'

'You can generally tell whether people are basically right for each other by whether they look good together, don't you think?' said Susannah. 'The idea never once occurred to me,' Geoffrey replied. 'It's not even occurring to me now. Do *we* look *good* together?'

She laughed. 'What do you think?' she said. He was still in a state of utter perplexity. She laughed again, and flapped the tea-towel in his face. 'Well, what do you think?' she asked. 'I still don't see how she can love him,' he said, 'however good they may or may not look together. Or however *tasty* he may or may not be. Not that he is.'

'He can do the *Times* crossword.'

'Oh, God.'

'Shall we go to bed?'

'Are you sure you wouldn't rather do the *Times* crossword?'

'We've only got a *Guardian.*'

'Won't that do instead?'

'For some reason, it doesn't seem to count the same.'

'I suppose we'll just have to go to bed then.'

'Oh, by the way, I told Nicola she could come and stay here, if this situation doesn't get sorted out pronto. If she really has to leave.'

'Well, *by the way*, I think that was rather unilateral of you.'

'What else could I do?'

Geoffrey heaved a sign and looked at her. 'Let's just assume,' he said, 'that the situation *will* get sorted out. After all, they're basically right for each other, as you pointed out. This is just a storm in a teacup.'

'Poor Nicola,' said Susannah sadly.

'Yes,' said Geoffrey, quite seriously. 'One way or another, poor Nicola.'

'And even poorer Jonathan,' said Susannah.

'Sod Jonathan,' said Geoffrey. He had had enough. 'Yes, well,' said Susannah, 'let's go to bed, shall we?' So they did.

# II

After all, Nicola told herself, alone under the covers, the flat silent around her, Jonathan absent in the country: he could not really, not surely, have meant it.

Of course, yes, he *meant* it: but only because he was mistaken. The thing that was wrong was a mistake, and she would, as soon as ever she could, discover this mistake and put it right: and then everything Jonathan had said, and meant, would be rescinded. As soon as ever she could!

He was bound to return on Sunday night, because the house agent was coming at his invitation on Monday morning: so she would see Jonathan again on Sunday night. Everything will be sorted out quite soon, thought Nicola: in just two days from now, this episode will all have become a bad dream, nothing more. Because otherwise, it is too bad to be true.

She dared now, just, to feel her way towards the contemplation of the scene of the previous night as if it might represent all of the truth, as if it might be an irreducible, however ugly, reality: as if Jonathan had not only meant what he had said, but had known what he meant: as if there were no mistake in the matter but her own — her own blindness to, ignorance of, Jonathan's true and natural feelings.

And now she allowed, she admitted, she was entirely bound to admit, that Jonathan might have meant what he said, might have known what he meant, and so wanted, not only truly, but justifiably, and with all his heart, to separate from her: yes, this unspeakable horror really was a logical possibility. Such events may truly occur. Love can grow cold, and become indifference – even dislike – even hatred.

She saw therefore that, whatever the truth of the matter, whether he meant or did not truly mean what he had said, Jonathan had become an absolute mystery to her. He was no longer the lover, comrade, companion she had known, but a frighteningly unreckonable creature as of faery. There can't be an awful lot of solicitors who seem like *that*, she thought; and she almost smiled. Susannah would have been proud of her.

# 12

'Is that all you're having? Just cereal? Don't you want some eggs and bacon? Goodness! Perhaps you'd like porridge. No? Well, I suppose you know best.'

'Of course he does. Of course he knows best. Truly to God, Sophie, you'd think he was five years old. Croissants, that's what he wants. That's what they eat for breakfast up in London. Croissants, French croissants. Should've got some in. What?'

'Don't be silly, Hugo. The very idea. Jonathan doesn't eat croissants. You don't eat croissants, do you, Jonathan? No, see, he's having some toast. Have some of that marmalade, darling, it's from the last lot I made for the WI stall, a bit runny, but you just have to eat it fast before it drips. Oh, but you used to *love* marmalade! I remember sending it to you at school. Didn't I? Well, I gave you some to take back with you. I remember. Marmalade. You used to insist on it.'

'Lot of rubbish.'

'What?'

'Lot of rubbish. Here. Listen to this.'

Hugo Finch, JP, began reading from the *Telegraph*. 'Senior back-benchers,' he began, 'are reported . . .' and so it went on: a further chapter in the gruesome, yet frequently hilarious, saga of the island people who had given the planet its common language and virtually all its games. What exactly were they working on now? None could truly say; many were the vain attempts to do so, but the question was beyond the scope of the merely human intelligence. Hugo concluded his reading.

'Splendid stuff,' said Jonathan, at the end of his tether. His father stared. 'What?' he said. 'What did you say?' He looked apoplectic.

'Splendid,' said Jonathan. 'Splendid!'

'Did you hear that? Did you hear what he said?'

'Yes, he's joking, Hugo. He doesn't mean it.'

'I'll tell you what he can do if he does: he can go straight back to London on the next train.'

'I've got a car.'

'Then bloody go and get into it and drive away, then! Splendid, he says! Splendid! Wants horsewhipping! Croissants! London! Horsewhipping!' Hugo flapped the newspaper straight with a loud *crack* and barricaded himself behind it. 'Croissants!' he muttered.

'Excuse me,' said Jonathan, getting up. He went out into the garden and walked about slowly, happily. It had taken years for him to learn that when they wind you up, the thing to do is wind them right back. Croissants – *French* croissants! Glorious! *Splendid!*

# 13

The splendour passed; Jonathan was possessed once more by the familiar demon whose dark oppressing wings enfolded his mind. He sat down on a garden seat and leaned back, closing his eyes against the bright spring sunshine, listening to the countryside sounds, trying, failing, to shun thought, recollection, reflection. Why this abiding darkness? Wasn't the worst over and done? Nicola, for all he now knew, might be gone, out of his sight, when he returned to London the following evening; he might even now be effectively free: free of all the terrible demands of that scrutiny, that intimacy, that sharing of the self. Free, and alone: to be alone was to be free.

Suddenly the weight of a human being fell on to the seat beside him and a voice loudly spoke to him. 'Ah! here you are!' It was his mother, whose approach had been silenced by the lawn across which she had advanced. Oh, *God*. No matter where one was, there was someone, some woman, peering into one's soul. It was intolerable. He had even (so he fancied) caught his secretary apparently at it. They peered into one's soul and left one naked and helpless.

He sat up. 'I was just thinking of going for a walk,' he said. 'Oh, but do stay for a moment now I'm here,' she said. 'Do tell me how Nicola is getting on. Such a pity she couldn't come with you, when the weather's so nice.' What a pity you are not married: have no children: aren't happier to be here: but see how tolerant we are, have always been; how tolerant, how patient.

All the younger generation seem to be the same, all living together without benefit of clergy. Of course they settle down in the end. Mostly. When would Jonathan's *end* arrive, though? It was taking such a very long time. And why no Nicola this weekend, after all? 'She always enjoys the garden so much, doesn't she?' she went on. 'Yes,' said Jonathan. 'I suppose she does.'

'So she's quite well, is she?' Not quite what we would have liked for Jonathan, *ideally*, but still, quite a nice girl. *Quite* a nice girl. Highly educated, of course; as they all are these days – funny, isn't it? 'Yes,' said Jonathan. 'She's fine.' 'Good,' said his mother. 'Well, you must make sure you bring her next time.' 'Yes,' said Jonathan. 'Sure thing.' Oh ho. You bet. Sorry, Ma.

# 14

On Saturday (while Jonathan basked, ate, walked, fumed, bashed croquet balls between hoops, and intermittently gloated) Nicola cleaned out all the kitchen cupboards. She cleaned the gas cooker, especially the oven. She even washed down all the paintwork, including the skirting boards, and she did two loads of washing, back to back. Then she washed her hair.

Mrs Brick had been in a few days before so there wasn't a lot to be done to the rest of the flat, but she did what there was, and a little more besides. On Sunday morning she polished the mirrors and the insides of the window panes and the television screen, and she washed all the china dogs and put them back on the mantelpiece in slightly different positions. After lunching off a tuna sandwich and an orange (Jonathan had overdone roast lamb and apple pie) she settled down to the ironing. She was getting through the time nicely.

She was just beginning on Jonathan's shirts (ah! Jonathan's shirts: God wears the exact same kind) when the telephone rang.

'Nicola? It's Lizzie.'

'Oh, Lizzie.'

'How are you?'

'I'm well, thanks, Lizzie. Are you?'

'Yes, I'm well too. Listen, darling, about next weekend.'

Oh God oh *God*.

'Ye-e-es?'

'Oh, dear, had you forgotten? I know we've messed you about so much, but we've just decided that we'll have to make it the weekend following after all. That's Easter, we thought we'd go down on Saturday and stay till Monday night. Will you be free? We can always defer it again if you're not but it would be nice if you were.'

'I'm not quite sure, I'll have to ask Jonathan.'

'Oh, of course. Could you ask him now so that we can settle it?'

'That's a bit tricky. He isn't here.'

'Not there? Well, ask him as soon as he comes in and ring me back.'

'I'm not sure . . . I'm not quite sure when he's going to be back, he may be rather late.'

'Goodness, has he gone away without you?'

'More or less.'

'Darling, you do sound odd. Is anything wrong?'

'Not really.'

'Darling, you sound as if you might be about to cry. Do tell me what has happened.'

'I can't.' She *was* about to cry. She had thought her tears were all shed. She had assured herself that once the ironing was done, and the evening had fallen, and Jonathan had returned, and she and he had talked, properly talked, to each other, everything would be normal again. Normal and nice. They would be a normal, nice couple again, and could make amicable arrangements again, and accept amicable invitations, as normal, like this one, from Lizzie and Alfred Ainsworth, to spend a weekend at their cottage (their poky little cottage where Jonathan kept banging his head and their little vixen of a daughter woke them up at five in the morning: but still. The scenery was divine).

She was on the verge of tears, as long as she tried to speak, because underneath her assurance that everything would (in just a few hours' time) return to niceness and normality was the black dread that it never would, and never could. No matter how beautifully she might iron Jonathan's shirts.

'Oh, Nicola, I don't like the sound of this. Listen, I'm going to come round, I have to fetch Henrietta from Battersea later on anyway. So you stay just where you are, I'm going to go straight out and get into the car and whizz straight round. I'll be with you before you know it.' And Lizzie hung up, just like that. Nicola flopped down on to the sofa and began to cry. She had a good fifteen minutes to shed her tears and dry them too, because Lizzie was coming all the way from Islington. Lizzie was one of those women who like to be at the scene.

But her tears did not last so long this time as they had before. If I can manage to finish ironing that shirt that I'd just started, she thought, looking across the room at the ironing board, by the time Lizzie gets here then that will mean that everything is going to be alright: and she went back to the ironing board, and ironed as quickly as she knew how; but it won't count, she admonished herself, if I don't do it properly. No skimping. And she was as careful as ever with the sleeves, the really awkward part. She finished a moment before the buzzer sounded, heralding Lizzie. Everything was going to be alright.

# 15

'Oh, Lizzie.'

'Oh, Nicola. Now what *is* all this about?'

'It's nothing really. You shouldn't have come.'

'I like that. Shall I go away again then?'

'No, stay and have some tea anyway.'

'Alright. Goodness, how clean and tidy it looks here.'

'Well, there's the ironing – sorry about that, I'd just started—'

'Goodness. Ironing as well. You are a treasure. I hope Jonathan's grateful. His shirts, I see.'

'Yes.'

'Lucky Jonathan.'

'Yes.'

'Oh, Nicola, do look at your face – oh – oh dear – oh, you *are* going to cry. Oh, Lord. Here, have you got a hanky? Oh dear. Poor Nicola. Now for Heaven's sake, darling, do tell Lizzie. What *is* the matter?'

'You're really the last person I should be telling,' said Nicola, between sobs. 'Jonathan would *kill* me.'

'Oh, would he *just*. Never mind him for the moment. Just *tell* me.'

It was dicey, alright. Susannah and Geoffrey were hers, but Alfred and Lizzie were Jonathan's. Well, Alfred, at any rate: he and Jonathan had known each other since school. On the other hand, Nicola having made their acquaintance had become rather more of an intimate of Lizzie's than Jonathan was of Alfred's.

But women were like that, as Alfred had remarked to himself – always getting together in corners and bonding: the phenomenon was clearly of evolutionary utility. He was quite content to leave them to it, as long as they weren't evidently hatching anything significant. Alfred loved women, in their place, and was at all times ready to assert that some of his female colleagues – he being at the bar – were very able indeed: *very*. Lizzie, of course, was not and never had been a colleague: *perish* the thought!

'Just let me make this tea first.' Nicola went into the kitchen and made the tea and brought it into the sitting room. Lizzie was looking at the china dogs. She picked up a pug. 'Is this Staffordshire?' she asked. 'Not exactly,' said Nicola. 'It's a proper eighteenth-century one. Derby. Jonathan gave it to me.'

'Don't cry again.'

'No, I won't.' She poured out the tea. 'Jonathan,' she said, 'wants us to split up. He's offered to buy me out.'

'How long has this been going on?'

'I've no idea. None at all. He just announced it, out of the blue, on Thursday night. Then he went to his parents for the weekend, straight from work on Friday. So I haven't had a chance to talk to him properly. I mean, he wouldn't discuss it on Thursday night. He just made his announcement and then clammed up. I was completely gobsmacked. I still am.'

'So am I.' And she was. They each drank some tea and Nicola began to eat a biscuit. 'And you really had no warning – no sign – beforehand?' asked Lizzie. 'No. Well, for all I know there were signs which I was too thick to see, but—'

'Tell me again exactly what he said and how.' Nicola obliged. 'Well,' said Lizzie, 'I must say that's quite the creepiest thing I've heard of in a long while. He should be strung up. It's an absolute outrage. And here you are, ironing his shirts! Nicola! What on *earth* are you thinking of?'

'Oh,' cried Nicola rather wildly, 'don't – don't be too hard on him – I don't know – we don't know – the whole story; he may be entirely justified – it's probably my fault completely – I just don't know, yet.'

'Only because he won't tell you. The pig, the pig, the absolute *pig*. Your fault! My God, that creep of a Jonathan should go down on his bended knees to you every day of his life – you should have seen the state he was in before he met you! You're the best thing that ever happened to him, and he doesn't deserve you, not for five seconds. You're well rid of him. He can go right back to where he was, and good riddance. Mournful putrid boring old Jonathan – he's had his last invitation to *my* house, if Alf wants to see him he can have lunch with him, *I'm* not having him about the place. These old bachelors, *really*! Useless! My God! *Men!*'

Nicola had begun to laugh: and then she began to cry, as well: and then she was crying, as if her heart might break, and not laughing at all. 'Oh, Nicola,' said Lizzie, patting her shoulder; 'he isn't worth it; he can't be; a man who can behave like that just isn't worth it. A man who makes you cry so is never worth your tears.'

'But I love him,' said Nicola. 'That's the trouble, you see. I really do love him.'

'You couldn't have found anyone less deserving,' said Lizzie.

'I didn't really try,' said Nicola; and in the midst of her tears she and Lizzie began to laugh. 'Oh, Christ,' said Lizzie; 'I mean, *Christ*.'

'Yes,' said Nicola. 'You never said a truer word.'

# 16

'Leaving aside the question of how you can love a rotten little creep like Jonathan in his present mode,' said Lizzie, 'not that women aren't absolutely famous for loving rotten little creeps—'

'Susannah says he's a prat,' said Nicola. 'So does Geoffrey. Do you think he's a prat?'

Lizzie considered. 'Prat,' she repeated. 'Yes, yes, he is *also* a prat. Quite certainly. How are Susannah and Geoffrey? Nice people.'

'They're well.'

'Bloody Jonathan. Your friends are wasted on him too. He doesn't *begin* to appreciate you. But look, the point is, Nicola sweetie, what exactly are you thinking of doing, apart from ironing Jonathan's shirts, which I absolutely *order* you not to do, my God, I can't *believe* it, bloody shirts, of all things, Jermyn Street too I'll bet, really *hard work*—'

'Yes, well . . .' said Nicola sadly. 'The point is,' said Lizzie, abandoning Jonathan's shirts as a bad job, 'what were you thinking of doing next, exactly? Now that the master has spoken.'

'Well,' said Nicola wanly, 'I was just – I was more or less expecting, or *hoping*, to see him tonight. I thought we might be able to talk, then. After he's been away from me for two days. And then, maybe, maybe we can sort it out. Maybe. I mean, I have to hope that. I have to hope.' She looked as if she might begin to cry again. 'Of course you do, my sweet,' said Lizzie quickly. '*Of course* you do. But *just in case* you don't. Just in case

Jonathan's decided to become a full-time complete professional dedicated creep and stick to his last, what then?'

'Well *then*,' said Nicola, 'I'll just have to clear off, won't I?'

'Not so fast,' said Lizzie. 'I mean, where will you go?'

'Oh,' said Nicola, 'Susannah says I can go there until I get sorted out.'

'That might take a while,' said Lizzie.

'Yes,' said Nicola hopelessly.

'You haven't really thought this through, have you?'

'No. I thought there wasn't really any point until I knew for certain that I had to.'

'It'll mean buying another flat, won't it?'

'Yes. Something really cheap, at that.'

'Quite.'

'Well . . .'

'The whole thing is a disgrace. You seem to have forgotten, you of all people, that this flat is actually *your* territory, morally speaking.'

Nicola pondered. 'Well, I suppose you're right,' she said uncertainly. 'You bloody bet I am,' said Lizzie. And as a matter of fact, she did have a point.

# 17

Nicola had moved into this flat in her late twenties; quite soon she would have been living here for exactly five years.

The flat was one of those lucky scores – such things can't be sought or even found serendipitously: they fall into the laps of those who manage to be in the right place at the right time by sheer accident. It had been one of the last of those dilapidated, rent-controlled Notting Hill flats, in a Victorian building whose 120-year lease was due when Nicola first moved in to expire a few years later.

The time arrived, the freehold of the building duly changed hands, and the new owners promptly notified each of the building's several tenants of his or her consequent options. Nicola, like her neighbours, was presented thus with the choice either of vacating her flat in return for a cash payment, or of purchasing the leasehold of the flat herself. Were she simply to remain as tenant the flat would be modernised and, as the house agents say, substantially upgraded; a new and quite unaffordable rent would thereafter be levied. Nicola's only possible choice – unable to afford to pay a higher rent, or to buy the leasehold – would have been to take the money and run; and she would have had to run rather a long way before finding another affordable flat – whether to rent, or to buy. It would not be so pretty nor so conveniently situated; she would certainly have been thrown into disarray for a period of several months or even years, had it not been for Jonathan.

Ah, Jonathan.

'Well, it all looks pretty straightforward,' he said. He was sitting on the sofa—the sofa that had been, the old wreck with its faded linen slipcover, when Nicola had been the sole inhabitant of this second-floor flat—reading through the letter from the new landlords, a property company with a Mayfair address. It had arrived in that morning's post; she'd read it walking up the street to the tube: horrible. She'd telephoned Jonathan at work and asked him to come round that evening and have a look.

They'd been going out for slightly less than a year: it seemed to be going quite beautifully: except for that edge of anxiety or even of fear—'can it last? are we actually—shall we—*do you really love me?*'—never articulated but always there, like a drone note which was silenced only during the act of love itself. But they lived, she lived, in hope, because it seemed, it just absolutely seemed to be the right, and just possibly, in so far as anything might be, the perfect thing: Jonathan and Nicola. A nice couple. Nicola and Jonathan—a couple: better off in every significant way together than alone: a couple, with their own jokes, their own memories, and their own impregnable psychic space. 'You couldn't pop round tonight could you? Just quickly?' 'Of course. No problem. Shall I bring something to eat?' 'No, it's alright. I think there's some food . . .' 'Well, we can always go out. I'll see you about sevenish.'

He'd arrived with some flowers for her, and a bottle of wine. 'Jonathan, you are nice.' 'Am I? Am I? Come here.' The dark blue smell of English serge: nothing else like it. Then the smell of Jonathan. Nothing else . . . 'Now, where's this letter of yours?'

Jonathan sitting on the old sofa, glass of wine in one hand, the letter in the other. 'Well, it all looks pretty straightforward.' 'I hoped it wasn't.' 'How do you mean?' 'I hoped there was a loophole.' 'No; you see . . .' 'So—' while she was chopping something, or peeling something, getting their dinner together; he had come into the kitchen, he was leaning against a workbench, watching her; she stopped what she was doing. She stared down at the chopping board. 'So . . . I don't really have any choice.' She felt completely hollow. It was a disaster. She was so perfectly happy, here. There was a view from the bedroom window of the communal gardens; you could hear children playing, shrieking, sometimes, with the joy that only children know. She picked up the vegetable knife again and stared at it as if ignorant of its function. 'I'm going to have to find somewhere else to live.' Slowly. The horror of it.

'You could buy the leasehold. It'd be a steal: as the sitting tenant you'd get something like a one-third reduction in the market price.'

'I *know*. I can't afford it even then. I've been doing the arithmetic all day. You know what I earn – it's just not possible.'

He thought for a moment. 'I suppose you're right,' he said. 'Well – look, what about getting on with the dinner, eh? I'm starving: I could get dangerous if we don't eat soon. Here, have some more of this.' He refilled her glass. 'Can I do anything?' 'It's okay. Alright. I'm nearly there.' Carry on; be brave.

After they'd sat down and begun to eat, he looked across at her. 'There is *one* other solution,' he said. She'd thought of it too, of course. She was almost sick, now, with apprehension, hoping almost to the point of panic that he might say what she yearned to hear, fearful almost to certainty that he wouldn't. 'What could that be?' She was wide-eyed with feigned innocence. What could that *possibly* be?

'I seem to be spending most of my free time here as it is, these days,' he said, in the tone of one making the most casual of remarks. 'Crawford Street's becoming simply a place where I keep my clothes.' Jonathan had a murky little flat in a Georgian house in Crawford Street, W1. He ate another mouthful. 'This is very good,' he said. 'You were saying.' 'Oh, yes. Well. I mean, it does seem an awful pity to let this place go.' Another mouthful. 'We've been happy here, haven't we?' She said nothing; she was too fearful, too overwhelmed with fear and terror and burgeoning hope. He looked up from his food, still holding his fork. 'Haven't we?' he repeated: and she saw anxiety, even fear, in his eyes too. 'Yes,' she said. 'Yes, we have. That is, I know *I* have. If you have too.' She was still terrified of what he might or might not say. 'Come here,' he said. 'You're too far away.' She got up and went to him, and he pulled her down on to his knee. He held her in his arms for a moment and then looked up at her. 'Do you think,' he said, 'that we might manage to make a go of living here together? All the time? Are you game for that?'

She smiled, she could not for the moment speak. She buried her face in the hollow between his neck and shoulder. 'Well?' he said. 'What do you think?'

# 18

Michael Gatling (very distantly related to the inventor of the gun) had just returned from taking his daughter Nicola to the station for the London train. His wife Elinor was still washing up the tea things.

'I don't know why he doesn't have done, and marry her,' he said, getting out the sherry. 'I suppose he will, in due course,' said Elinor, rattle, rattle. 'He's just running a little trial.' 'Bloody cheek,' said Michael. 'The trial's on the other foot, as far as I'm concerned. The nerve of these chaps.'

'Still,' said Elinor, 'at least she'll be able to keep the flat. Such a very charming place. It's a pity we couldn't help her more.'

'Tush,' said Michael. 'I'm only a poor civil servant. She hardly expected anything at all, she's more than grateful for the five thou'. So she should be.'

'Ah, my baby. My last child. How sad it all is, somehow.'

'Honestly, Nellie, you do talk some awful rot. 'It's fathers who are meant to be sentimental, not mothers. Here, stop washing up and drink this.' He handed her a glass of amontillado. She sat down. She was frowning slightly. 'I do hope they'll be happy,' she said. 'We must look out something for a housewarming present, once it's all settled.'

'Never mind that,' said Michael. 'Wait until it's time for a wedding present.' 'Just something very small,' said Elinor. 'I might go into Brighton this week and have a poke around the junk shops.' 'Alright,' said Michael. 'But something *truly* small. They might feel we're putting the pressure on, otherwise.'

'Oh, but we wouldn't dream of doing that,' said Elinor. 'Would we?' 'Not us,' said Michael. 'Not card-carrying moderns like us. *Nevertheless*, I don't know why he doesn't have done, and *marry* her.'

Nicola, travelling back to London in a second-class compartment on the Brighton–Victoria line, was almost delirious with happiness. It had all happened so fast – just a few days ago she had been holding that appalling letter in her hand, her heart beating with fear and dismay: now with a turn of the kaleidoscope all the pieces of her life had been rearranged into a different and more beautiful pattern. Jonathan and she were going jointly to purchase the leasehold of the Notting Hill flat; they would own a half share each, because her total contribution to the cost would take into consideration the discount due to her as the sitting tenant. Her parents having so magnificently chipped in with £5,000 she should be able quite easily to borrow the remainder of her share from the bank: you could almost hear the *click* as everything fell into place.

'Well – I might as well put Crawford Street on the market straight away,' Jonathan had said before leaving her, that night of the letter. He was going to do nicely out of Crawford Street, which he'd bought at the very beginning of the property boom. 'You'd better wait until I see my parents,' Nicola had replied. 'I don't know that I'll be able to manage my share without them.' 'Oh, everything will work out,' said Jonathan airily. He was so very much richer than she: he could afford to be airy. But now everything had in fact worked out; it was almost magical.

'Come round to Crawford Street tomorrow night after work,' Jonathan said when she telephoned him with the good news after reaching home that evening. 'And we'll decide which pieces of furniture we want to keep from here. Then we might go out for some dinner.' And so she had; and so their common life had properly begun.

'Are you *sure*?'

'Of *course* I am. Old mahogany wardrobes like that are almost priceless these days. A real *armoire*.'

'Well, if you say so. I'm sure I didn't pay more than £50 for it.'

'Well, you can add another nought, now. At least.'

'I'll be blowed.'

'Oh, really?'

'Nicola!'

# 19

And so Jonathan did all the conveyancing, and Nicola disposed of all her tatty old furniture, and they had someone in to sand and seal the sitting-room floorboards, and they bought a discreetly magnificent new bed, Empire style, in the Liberty's sale, and Jonathan and all his chattels moved in. He opened a half bottle of Bollinger and poured each of them a glass, and in due course another, and then he lobbed the empty bottle into the waste paper basket. 'And you won't get any more where that came from,' he said, 'until we've finished painting this room: is that understood?' 'Yes, Master,' said Nicola. Bliss!

'I say, Lizzie, where are you?'

'I'm here, where should I be?'

'Oh, jolly good.'

'Give me a kiss.'

'Alright. Here.'

'You smell of whisky.'

'Well spotted. I ran into Jonathan Finch just as I was leaving chambers. He'd been in conference with Jessop. That Lloyd's thing.'

'Oh, yes, indeed, that Lloyd's thing. Is there even one of you who hasn't got a piece of the action?'

'No, shouldn't think so. It's going to pay for all the school fees for the rest of the century, and beyond.'

'It's an ill wind.'

'Right. So anyway, we went for a drink.'

'Thrilling.'

'No, listen. I've got some gossip for you.'

'Never. Stuffy stagnant old Jonathan? Never.'

'Hang about. He is stuffy and stagnant no longer. He's full of beans, you never saw the like. Transformation.'

'Oh – discovered his hidden powers, has he?'

'You could say so. Tantamount. He's just bought half a flat in Notting Hill.'

'Say no more.'

'Listen, try to be serious. We're talking about my old mate Finch, J. H. God, we went through purgatory together.'

'If you ask me he's still there.'

'But I'm *not* asking you, I'm trying to *tell* you. God, but you do try a chap's patience. Now: who do you think owns the other half of the aforementioned Notting Hill flat?'

'Don't tell me, let me guess.'

'You never will, so I shall. Note my grammar, by the way.'

'Yes, very well, noted. Alright, so tell me: who *is* the abovementioned co-owner?'

'Only a sweet young thing called Nicola Gatling.'

'Like the gun.'

'Yes, like the gun.'

'How do you know she's sweet?'

'He showed me a photo.'

'He *what*?'

'A photo. Sweet. Dark hair, thin face. Intelligent. Thirtyish.'

'He had a *photo*?'

'Yes, why not? Just a small one. In his wallet.'

Lizzie left the stove and sat down and began to laugh. 'Good Lord,' she said. 'He's serious.'

'Well of course he is. He's bought this flat with her. There they are, living in sin together at this very moment. So there.'

'Wonders will *never* cease.'

'Exactly. If only we could all bear that in mind – oh and by the way, I said he should bring her round for a meal some evening, okay?'

'Oh, that was good of you.'

'Yes, well, what could I do?'

'What indeed.'

'Important step in a chap's life.'

'Considering it's taken him so long to make it.'

'Well, some of us are slow starters. Not the chap's fault.'

'No, nothing is ever one's fault. It's still one's responsibility to sort it out, though.'

'So he *has* sorted it out.'

'Apparently.'

'So anyway, let's have them round. Don't you want to take a look at this Nicola?'

'Yes. Sure. Have you got the number?'

'No. But you could telephone him at work.'

'Write down the name of the firm then, I'll never remember it. On the calendar there. Only I can't do anything for a few weeks, I'm up to my ears.'

Lizzie was an independent television producer, a fairly discernible operator. But once in a while she cooked the dinner, as tonight, for therapy. She got up and went on with it. 'Okay,' said Alfred, who was madly curious to see the woman in the case. 'I'll remind you.' 'You sweetie you,' said Lizzie. 'Now you'd better buzz up and see Henrietta while you've got the chance, or she'll be asleep. You could ask Marie-Laure to come down here for a moment if you will.'

'Oh, yes, Harry. Has she been good today?'

'Ish,' said Lizzie. 'Just ish. From what I hear. But it's better than nothing.'

'She's a girl of spirit,' said Alfred proudly. 'I like a girl with spirit.' And he went up to Henrietta, and read her *The Fox and the Grapes*.

# 20

The sitting-room windows faced south, and gave a view of a terrace of stucco-fronted Victorian houses like the one they inhabited, and beyond these the tops of trees growing in the communal gardens: it looked, especially in the evening, like a stage set for an urban operetta. They'd just finished painting the sitting-room walls midsummer-sky-blue, with the cornices picked out in white. 'We're pretty good, aren't we?' said Jonathan. But he'd decided to get a professional in to do the ceiling. They sat down on the sofa, the rather good old one which they'd bought at auction and which had cost them an arm and a leg – how appropriate – and Jonathan opened another half bottle of champagne.

'It might be nice to do something about the bathroom,' he said. 'No,' said Nicola. 'I'm cleaned out.' 'Let me give it to you for a present,' said Jonathan. 'It can be your Christmas present.' 'But that's not for months and months,' said Nicola. 'An early present,' said Jonathan. And so one way or another the flat was, after all, substantially upgraded, and pretty good it looked, too, in a laid-back, understated, Notting Hillish way. Part of the upgrading of the bathroom was the latest and best thing in showers, with very shiny taps and hoses and five different kinds of spray. Bliss!

'Are we doing anything on Sunday?'
'I don't know, are we?'
'Not if you don't think so.'
'We'll ask Guy. We've probably promised him something

and forgotten it. He'll remember. Guy!'

'What is it?'

'Did we fix anything for Sunday?'

'No, Saturday. Roller skating, remember?'

'Oh, yes. You bet. Right. That's all then, you can go away again if you like.'

'No, I'll stay, in case you're talking about something interesting.'

'We're not. We're only talking about Sunday.'

'What about Sunday?'

'Nicola's asked us to go over to Notting Hill for lunch.'

'Why?'

'She wants us to see her posh new flat and her posh new co-habitant.'

'Cor.'

'So since we're not doing anything else, we will.'

'Oh, Susannah, must we?'

'Can I stay at home, Mum?'

'Yes we must. No you can't.'

'Oh!'

'Oh!'

'You *like* Nicola.'

'But there's *him*.'

'You hardly *know* him.'

'I don't *want* to.'

'We needn't stay long.'

'We won't.'

'We'll see.'

'I don't want to go. I want to stay here.'

'You can't stay here alone, my treasure. We'll go somewhere nice afterwards. We might go to a film. We'll see what's on.'

'Promise?'

'Promise.'

'Whizzy!'

# 21

'Well, that was painless enough wasn't it?' said Susannah. She and Geoffrey and Guy were in the car on their way from Notting Hill to the South Bank to see *The Navigator* as per the agreed *quid pro quo*. Guy's behaviour throughout the luncheon had been exemplary; even Geoffrey's reluctance had been dissipated. 'Blokes who can come up with plonk like that,' said he, having drunk Jonathan's claret liberally, 'are OK by me.' Susannah (who was driving) frowned but said nothing. She was doing Hyde Park Corner.

'What did *you* think of him?' she asked Guy. 'He's alright,' the child replied. 'I don't think he's met anyone of my age before. He's fairly nice.' 'I think so too,' said Susannah. 'And his wine is better still,' said Geoffrey. 'So we're all happy,' said Susannah. 'Especially Nicola,' said Geoffrey unexpectedly. 'Yes,' said Susannah. 'Isn't she? It almost breaks my heart to look at her.' 'Why does it break your heart?' asked Guy, genuinely puzzled. 'Ah, if I could only tell,' she said. 'But I canna.' This impasse was breached by their having arrived at their destination, so they parked and hurried inside just in time to buy the tickets and get themselves settled in before the great work commenced, once again, its *déroulement*.

Much later that night when Guy had gone to bed, 'What did you really think of him?' Susannah said to Geoffrey. 'Now that we've had a good long look.'

Geoffrey was catching up with the Sunday papers – 'Not

that there's a bloody thing worth reading in these rags, except for some of the political commentary', he looked up, nonplussed. 'Who?' he said. 'You mean Buster? A genius. Haven't I always said so?'

'Not Buster Keaton, you fool. I mean Jonathan.'

'Ah, yes. I see. Jonathan. Well, as I said, his liquor's first-rate. More than that I cannot tell.'

'Oh, do make an effort.'

'What do want me to say? He's just another lawyer, isn't he, just another cunning, cautious, conservative, overpaid jackass. Not my kinda guy, but why should he be? I'll be happy to drink his wine whenever the occasion arises.'

'You're the limit!' said Susannah. 'Of all the snobbish, prejudiced, narrow-minded—'

'Ah, you girls,' Geoffrey interrupted. 'You do love a man of means, don't you?'

'Naturally.'

'You can't buck biology.'

'What do you mean?'

'You're programmed to admire these good-provider types. Can't think what you're doing with the likes of me.'

'No, I must try and work that out some time.'

'The answer may shock you.'

'I shouldn't be surprised.'

'Can one be shocked but not surprised?'

'Oh, belt up!' She threw the colour supplement at him and he replied with the review section. Soon the newspapers were in a state of disarray exactly analogous to the world they chronicled.

# 22

'There, what did I tell you? Was I right or was I not?'

'What did you tell me?'

'Transformation. Stagnant no more. Sweet young thing. All systems go.'

'Alright, you were right. So far. Although *young* isn't quite the word, she's almost as old as I am.'

'You're young.'

'You're sweet.'

'There you are then. *And I was right.*'

'I think she's got more brains than you gave her credit for.'

'Oh, brains, yes of course, isn't it extraordinary how you've all got brains, these days. It must be a mutation.'

'If only men could catch it.'

'You don't catch mutations. They just arrive. Acts of God.'

'Dear old God. He's certainly done Jonathan a favour. I hope the man is grateful.'

'I doubt if Jonathan believes in God.'

'That's too bad.'

'Why?'

'No one to be grateful to. Therefore no gratitude. Dangerous vacuum in the circumstances.'

'I don't believe in God either, and neither do you. Do we have a dangerous vacuum?'

'No, but we're different.'

'How?'

'We've got Henrietta.'

'Oh, yes. We certainly have.'

'Nicola was very good with Henrietta, did you notice? I did try to persuade her to go to bed before they arrived but it was useless.'

'Whatever happened to obedience?'

'Obedience? Oh, that went the way of – well, what? – liberty bodices, and codliver oil – and the rest – years ago.'

'Seems a mistake to me.'

'I can't personally see there's much to be said for codliver oil, *or* liberty bodices.'

'Or obedience?'

'The problem is that we're all too worn out these days to instil it, I'm afraid. Anarchy is so much easier.'

Alfred looked almost grim, but then his expression brightened. 'She'll have to learn it at school,' he said. 'Yes,' said Lizzie, 'so she will. That's the best place for it. That's one of the things school is *for*.'

'The one where she's going, anyway,' said Alfred. 'Yes, that's right,' said Lizzie. 'She'll get the hang of it quick enough, from all I can remember.' And for a moment she looked almost grim herself. 'Poor little sprog,' she said.

'Nonsense,' said Alfred. 'We all need something to cut our teeth on.'

'She's actually quite a good child, on average,' said Lizzie. 'Good enough, as it were.'

'I should dashed well hope so,' said Alfred. 'She'd soon hear about it from me if she weren't.'

'I expect she knows that.'

'Good.'

# 23

Jonathan was driving back from Gloucestershire, with the sun setting behind him, Radio Four wittering away from the dashboard. He was about half way home when he got caught in a tail-back, and the wittering became intolerable. He switched over to tape and stuck in the first cassette he was able to lay his hand on. It was a bootlegged talking book which he vaguely remembered some BBC employee friend of Nicola's having given to her. 'It might be handy for long journeys,' she'd told him, putting it in the glove box.

The story began, and went on: some footling tale about some shop assistants in an antipodean department store, fretting about their wombs and their wardrobes and other empty spaces – ye gods! No wonder women were for ever peering into one's soul! They were compensating for their own innate emptiness. Perhaps, truly, they had no souls of their own. Jonathan was altogether prepared to consider this proposition. Of course no one knew what a soul was, or even that such a thing objectively existed, but it was fairly certain, thought Jonathan, that women did not have souls of the same order as those of men. Jonathan was much too stricken and angry to be bothered to think straight.

By tea-time on Sunday afternoon he'd had more than enough: his father's expostulations, his mother's irrelevancies, the whole horror of having been born, there, to them and of having had, therefore, to experience just what he had experienced: the burden of its remembrance and the agony of its continuation, even now, so long as they all should live: the banality and the pain: neither was more endurable than the other, and the admixture was poisonous. He did not want to *be* Jonathan Finch, but he was nevertheless condemned to it, through no fault of his own.

Just as he was packing up the last of his things in the holdall, just before tea, his mother had come into his room.

'Excuse me, darling,' she'd said – her diffidence was not her least irritating characteristic: 'I just thought – look – I have something to show you – here.' And he'd turned from the chest of drawers, hairbrush in hand: 'Yes? What is it?'

'It's your great-grandmother's lovely ring,' she'd said. 'I've just had it cleaned. You can't be too careful with these old settings. Look, hasn't it come up beautifully?'

Jonathan obliged her so far as to inspect it. He wasn't interested in such things, but it looked even to him fairly impressive: a pigeon's blood ruby encircled by diamonds. 'Yes,' he said. 'It's beautiful.'

Sophie was trying to choose the right words. 'I've never worn it,' she said. 'Somehow, rubies are not my stone. I have the wrong colouring.' This was correct. She, like Jonathan and his sister Clarissa, was very fair. 'Issa's been after me for years to let her have it,' she went on, 'but I've always meant to give it to you for an engagement ring for the girl you decide to marry. That is if you'd like it. If you think she'd like it. And then I was just thinking the other day, whoops, what if Jonathan were to pop the question and go out and buy a ring, never knowing I meant him to have this – wouldn't that be perfectly silly? I should have offered it to you years ago! What a duffer I am. Anyway, no harm done, I hope. Here, darling. Please take it. Or I'll mind it for you, which-ever you prefer. But as long as you know it's here. I'll have a codicil put on my will so that it goes to you anyway, just in case anything happens to me before you should get engaged. It's an awfully good stone, you know, a pigeon's blood ruby is very rare, and the setting of course is antique, it really is worth quite a lot of money, I was surprised – I'm sure any girl would love it.'

Jonathan could have wept. Irritation – even hostility – vexation, sorrow, shame, guilt, gratitude and, finally, love, helpless, unarticulated, endless, all violently clashed together in his miserable heart. He gazed down at the ring, which still lay, innocent, invulnerable, in the palm of his mother's outstretched hand. 'Thank you,' he said. He looked up at her. There were tears in his eyes. 'That's really—' but he could say no more, he was afraid of crying, and furious, furious at the prospect, furious with himself, furious with life, which could turn such tricks. 'It's nothing,' said Sophie hastily, 'it's nothing at all. I've always meant you to have it. Shall I keep it here for you? It's on the insurance, you wouldn't have to worry.'

'Yes,' said Jonathan, his tears now suppressed. 'Please. That would be truly kind.' 'Oh, it's nothing,' she said. 'It's a pleasure.' There was no need to say exactly how her kindness might be repaid, and Jonathan felt a new anguish, a new guilt, in his secret knowledge of the awful unlikelihood of making this repayment in the near or even distant future. The ring might glitter here in the darkness for years, even decades, until with his mother's death it came (like a homing pigeon) to him. He suddenly remembered another thing about pigeons. That they mated, so he'd heard, for life.

Later on, with tea and all its *malheurs* – 'Oh, do have another scone, won't you? I made them just for you' – 'I suppose you're much too busy up in London to get down here more often than you do – of course you have better things to do of a Saturday than play cricket, why the bloody hell should you? Let the village team go to the devil, who cares these days? I suppose you'd rather be *pumping iron*, isn't that what they call it, in some foul gymnasium, with a lot of blacks, and women wearing silver leotards. I'll tell Anstruther he can forget having your services this season, or any other I dare say. *Sic transit, sic transit,* who the hell cares' – with all this, Jonathan's mind was delivered from the state which had been induced by Sophie's present of the ring; by the time he was on the point of leaving – 'Back to London, then! Sooner you than me!' – he suffered merely from the usual symptoms. Gloucestershiritis, he and Issa (in the days before they'd grown so slowly, but finally, apart) had used to call it. But it had become with the passing years more virulent and intense: then it had been a bad cold, but now it was influenza.

And he was out of the county altogether before it was revealed to him that, of course, his mother, in showing him, then giving him, the ring, had managed – and had this been her purpose? – once more to peer, however inconclusively, into his soul.

Just as he had turned the key in the ignition she had frantically tapped on the window. 'Wait!' she cried. 'I almost forgot. Wait!' She ran inside and returned with a carrier bag and signalled to him to open the window. 'Marmalade,' she said. 'For Nicola. With my love, of course. Yes, I know you don't care for it, any longer, but I'm sure she'd like to have some. Home-made is so much nicer. There!' Marmalade, for Nicola. With any luck, by the time he got back to the flat, if not long before, she'd be gone.

# 24

'I mean, I think it's a bit too cool altogether,' Lizzie declared, 'for Jonathan to ask you to leave this flat. You were here first.'

'Well, he did say I could buy him out if I liked,' said Nicola miserably. 'But I can't afford to.'

'Exactly!' cried Lizzie. 'As he perfectly well knows.'

Nicola looked down at the rug. It was time it was shampooed again: perhaps she could do that next weekend. Then she remembered; her misery redoubled. 'The thing is, we never – that is, I never – foresaw this situation when we first bought the flat. I mean, how could I? I thought we'd simply go on living here happily ever after, until it got too small.' Oh, vain dreams! Marriage, children, a four-bedroomed house in a slightly cheaper part of London: that was the only alteration ever foreseen by Nicola.

'Ye-e-es,' said Lizzie. 'Of course.' It was difficult to go on. Nicola was too nice for her own good; it was up to her friends to be tough for her. 'I'll accept that even now you still love the horrid pig, even to the point of trying to oblige him in every whim – up to and including the whim of sending you packing; but I really don't see why you should put yourself out particularly. It's very noble and generous of Susannah to offer you a home *pro tem.* and I can see that it would be stylish, in a way, for you simply to vanish from Jonathan's deluded sight without further ado: but if I were you I'd stay exactly where you are for just as long as convenient. Of course he may well stick to his guns, but he can't force you out. If I know anything about it he'd have to take it to court and you can be sure he doesn't want to do *that*.'

None of these considerations had previously entered Nicola's mind; they altered the whole picture. She stared at the empty grate. 'Court,' she said wonderingly. 'Would he really do that?' 'I've just told you,' said Lizzie, 'not if he can possibly avoid it. So I think you should take all the time you like. If it really does come to separating.' She took Nicola's hand. 'But look – don't think about that until you really must. And in the meantime, hang in here. Jonathan absolutely does not have the right to order you off the premises in this way, whatever he might wish, and that is a fact. Of course it will be awkward, but that's his problem. I suppose he's bunked off to the spare room, has he? Of course. Well I just hope the bed in there is bloody uncomfortable.' 'It is rather hard,' said Nicola woefully. 'Good!' said Lizzie. 'No electric blanket either, I hope?' 'No,' said Nicola. 'There is a hot water bottle. But I don't suppose he'd use it.'

'Oh, but I do like the sound of Jonathan on a hard bed with a hot water bottle for company. It doesn't leak, by any chance, does it?' 'I don't think so,' said Nicola. 'Well, that can be fixed,' said Lizzie. 'Where is it?' 'Oh, no, you mustn't!' cried Nicola. Only then did she see that Lizzie was not perfectly serious. 'Oh, Lizzie,' she cried. 'You're teasing me. You think I'm stupid, don't you?'

'I know you're not,' said Lizzie. 'But I do think you're soft.' Nicola looked hopeless. 'It will all work out somehow,' Lizzie now unexpectedly found herself saying. 'You'll see; truly it will.' Why am I saying this? she asked herself. She felt ashamed for saying something she could not mean.

'But whatever you do' she went on, 'don't, please, iron any more of those sodding shirts. Promise?'

Nicola looked wretchedly down at the rug again and then back at Lizzie. 'I'll try not to,' she said. 'I'll try.' 'You're incorrigible,' said Lizzie. 'A hopeless case. Wherever did you come from? A nineteenth-century orphanage?' 'No,' said Nicola. 'I haven't even that excuse.' 'Poor darling,' said Lizzie. 'Give me a hug. There. It will all work out somehow, you'll see.' How could she say this? Oh dear.

'And now I really must eff off,' she said. 'It's time I fetched Henrietta from the Carringtons. Do you remember meeting them? She's been playing with Fergus. They're cousins, you see; Louisa is Alf's sister. Anyway, look, I'll be in touch. But telephone me whenever you want – you've got my work number, haven't you? And *please, don't* iron those shirts, I *beg* you.'

# 25

Nicola was ironing Jonathan's shirts, and she was thinking: remembering: racking her brains: she was trying as hard as she could to recollect the past and to perceive the truth.

There had been those moments of lesser dread which might have warned her of a possible greater such moment to come: but she had not been warned; she had dismissed them because they had made no sense. They had been anomalies in the narrative as she understood it: as she had believed (or had assured herself) Jonathan understood it too. Nevertheless, yes, there had been those moments when Jonathan – overtired, she had thought, under strain; for he did work so hard; he was an ambitious lawyer approaching mid-career; he spent most of his waking hours unpicking Gordian knots, and then tying, with infinite concentration, yet others – when Jonathan – yes: would stare at her as if to say: who are you; why are you here? Moments when he seemed not only not to know her, but not to want to know her: moments when the light they had seemed to bask in was suddenly occluded, and their solid world became a sham: moments when she saw for a fact that they were two fearful strangers.

And she'd get up, go away, do something in another room; pretending that nothing was wrong, nothing at all, but nevertheless, pretend as she might, she was wracked with dismay; she was possessed by a black and mysterious dread. And later on – to be sure! – nothing, after all, *was* wrong, nothing at all: Jonathan would come to her just as he'd used to be: I say, what are you doing in here? Oh, don't do that now – come and watch *Forty Minutes* – come for a walk – let's catch that film at the Electric – Nicola, where are you?

And Nicola had described none of this to Lizzie or even to Susannah: it was not a phenomenon one could easily describe, even to oneself. And even less could she have described or even mentioned that scene, which might amount to almost nothing after all, of a few months past, that very tiny scene, more of an entr'acte, but nevertheless – this was very superior stagecraft – disturbing, chilling: a scene which had left her more truly, more deeply, in dread, and more strenuously determined to carry on, bravely: for almost surely, after all, nothing was wrong.

Jonathan had been half sitting up in bed, reading a book, waiting for her: she was still occupied at the dressing table. She was wearing the white satin nightdress: she could remember each detail (you see) quite clearly: another present from Jonathan. This was the time of the day – last thing before bed – when she took the pill. She was looking at the packet as she spoke. She said, I'm going to have to stop taking this in about six months' time. And he'd said, oh really, why? And she'd said, you have to stop after a while and do something else, otherwise there are certain risks. Do you want me to do something, he said; and she said no, after all, there isn't really anything acceptable that a man can do. What's the alternative? he asked. That's where it gets rather tricky, she said; and she explained all the alternatives and why each was tricky. Which only leaves, she finished, the Roman Catholic method. But we're not Roman Catholics, he had said. She had laughed. And actually, she had said, none of the Roman Catholics I know use that method either. Not unless they actually want to have children. 'Ah,' he said. 'Well, we don't actually want to have children either. So you'd better choose

76

one of the other Roman Catholic methods.' And he went back to his book.

She felt as cold as steel when she got into bed; her heart was frozen. He put down the book and switched off the lamp and they lay silent in the darkness. He won't touch me, she thought. I don't even want him to. After a while he reached out and very slowly, carefully, began to untie the bows which secured the shoulder straps of the white satin nightdress, and then very slowly, carefully, he began, as if nothing were wrong, to make love to her; and after a while, nothing, for the moment, perhaps at all, *was* wrong.

# 26

'What are you doing in here?'

'I'm just trying to make some room in this cupboard.'

'Why?'

'For Nicola. In case she comes to stay for a bit.'

'Oh, Lord. Can't she leave her things on the floor like everyone else?'

'No of course she can't. Look, if I take these shelves out, and you put up a rail, she could use this to hang up her clothes.'

'Who says I'm going to put up a rail?'

'God does. I'll buy one tomorrow and you can put it up when you get back from the poly.'

'The *university*, you mean. She might not even come. A waste of a good rail and what's worse my time.'

'No, it'll be dead handy whatever happens. Now all these things – have we got any more of those wooden boxes we had?'

'You mean those wine crates? There might be a few under the stairs.'

'Could you be a darling and look? Then I can put all this junk in them and we'll be all set to go.'

'Oh, Lord.'

'You'd be lost for words without the Lord, wouldn't you?'

'Well we all would; the whole thing you know was His idea in the first place. *In the beginning was the Word, and the Word was with God, and the Word was God.*'

'Isn't that beautiful.'

'Yes, and since beauty is truth and truth beauty it is therefore also *true*.'

'So if you could just fetch me those crates. And I'll just look out some sheets. I'll have to pinch some of Guy's.'

'Toil and trouble, toil and trouble. Bubble on.'

'I think I'll just telephone Nicola now quickly and make sure she's alright.'

'Are we meant to be getting any supper tonight or are you too busy with Nicola?'

'Yes, there are some bangers in the fridge. Perhaps when you've got me those crates you could get them out and put them under the grill. I'll be there in a minute.'

Susannah picked up the telephone receiver and Geoffrey with a look of helpless resignation left the room. Ten minutes later she came into the kitchen. 'Well, that's alright,' she said.

'What is?'

'Nicola.'

'Oh, all sorted out again, is she? That's good. We needn't bother about that rail.'

'No, she isn't *sorted out*. She hasn't seen him yet, he hasn't returned from the country yet. But she seems to feel that she should stay put for a few days at least.'

'Of course she should.'

'Well, *I* wouldn't.'

'She hasn't got your proud and fiery nature. Anyway, just so long as we needn't bother about that rail.'

'We need. She might change her mind. She probably will. She might suddenly become proud and fiery: I hope in fact that she will.'

They were interrupted by Guy. 'I'm hungry.' 'Good, I'm just getting supper now.'

'Can we have chips?'

'Look in the freezer and see if there are any.' He did; there were; Susannah turned on the oven. 'I wish I could learn to ride,' said Guy, not for the first time. 'I'll have to see if we can afford it,' said Susannah. 'You said that before, but you haven't.' 'I will. I'll put it in my diary.' 'We probably can't,' said Geoffrey. 'It doesn't cost very much,' said Guy in a small voice. Susannah more or less made up her mind then that, cost what it might, Guy should learn to ride; and quite right too.

# 27

Jonathan glanced up at the sitting-room windows and saw the light. So she was still there. Steeling himself, he crossed the street and ascended the stairs to the second floor.

Nicola was on the point of dishing up some tinned soup when she heard Jonathan's key turning in the lock. She waited – terrified – for his entrance; in a moment, he was before her in the kitchen doorway.

'Hello.'

Jonathan ever so slightly shrugged. 'I wasn't sure you'd still be here,' he said.

'Where should I be?'

He shrugged again and turned away.

'Would you like some soup?'

'Is there enough?'

'I'll just make some more toast.'

He sat down as if only half willingly and she put the soup in front of him and then sat down herself. He picked up the spoon and idly took an experimental mouthful. Cream of celery.

Now that he was here, speechlessly drinking soup, Nicola all at once perceived that he was even less able to manage their dreadful new situation than she. Her fear abated and she began to feel a sort of pity. After a moment, 'I was hoping,' she said carefully, 'that we might talk.'

'Talk? About what?'

'About what has happened. About this decision you've come

to. I was hoping that you might be ready to explain yourself.'

There was a silence, and she dimly saw that the wretchedness within him which had brought about the dreadful announcement of Thursday night had engendered a black fog which obscured all paths to enlightenment: the very fact of his acting and speaking as he had done indicated an incapacity for any other kind of discourse. The black fog seemed to creep through her own pores; soon she would be as incapacitated as he. What in God's name ailed him?

'I told you: there's nothing *to* explain, further to what I've said already.'

She might now have become angry; but perhaps because she was so exhausted, depleted by anguish and fear and interrupted sleep, she could feel only a kind of impatience, and still that ghostly pity. In any case it seemed that nothing she could do or say might touch his recalcitrance.

'It won't *do*, Jonathan,' she said very gravely. 'Really it won't.'

He thought about this. 'It will have to *do*,' he said. 'It's all I've got.'

'Well, we'll see, shall we?' she said. Suddenly her impatience broke its bounds. 'We'll see, if it's all you've got. I'll be here for the rest of the week at least, whether you like it or not, so I dare say we'll run into each other once in a while if not every single morning and every single evening. You may find you've got more to say after all – I hope for your sake that you do. If you truly haven't then I'm well rid of you, because in that case, it looks as if you've had a brain transplant, and I hope it didn't cost much because if it did then you've been ripped off. I should see the Trading Standards Officer if I were you.'

Oh, if only Susannah had heard her. Or Lizzie. Or best of all, both of them. How they would have cheered! As it was, Nicola was cheering herself. Where had it all come from? Hallelujah!

Jonathan was stunned. His eyes were full of incredulity and

84

he was speechless. Nicola got up and put the dirty dishes in the sink. 'Could you put all your clothes in the spare room cupboard,' she said, 'and any other bits and pieces you need from the bedroom. So that you won't need to disturb me more than necessary. For the rest of the time that I'm here I'll stay out of your way as much as I can, without overdoing it, naturally. Perhaps you could see to your clothes now – I want to have an early night.'

Still speechless, Jonathan stumbled to his feet and awkwardly left the room; Nicola, catching sight of his dazed expression as he did so, would for two pins have run to him and hugged and consoled him. My own love, she might have said, *what is wrong?* But she sensed that it would have been futile: that the bewilderment on his face was belied by the murderous coldness which still quite evidently gripped his heart. So she turned instead to the sink and began to wash up.

# 28

He was in the doorway again; he made an awkward gesture. It was still difficult to address her. 'I've – moved my things,' he said. 'The coast is clear.' One might have thought that it was she who had asked him to leave. 'Good,' she said. 'I've made some tea, will you have some?' He came in and sat down once more. He was carrying a plastic bag which he put on the table. 'My mother sent you this,' he said. 'Oh?' 'I believe it's some marmalade,' he said. 'From the latest batch.' 'How kind,' said Nicola, opening the bag. 'You haven't told them, then?'

'Told them what?'

'That we're no longer in a shared marmalade situation. That you've given me notice. That I'm out of their lives.' No need to pile it on, though.

'I thought it best to wait, until—'

'Oh, yes. Until I've actually gone. Very circumspect. Meanwhile I've got some marmalade. It seems like false pretences, but still. I must remember to take it with me when I go.' She looked inside the carrier bag. There was something else there as well, wrapped in damp-looking newspaper. She withdrew it – an awkward, very light cone-shaped parcel. 'What's this?' she said.

'I don't know. She didn't mention anything else – it all happened at the last minute, as I was leaving.'

Nicola unwrapped the damp newspaper to discover a small and exquisit posy of early spring flowers – the sort of posy that only a woman with a garden can ever produce, lovelier by far than anything from even the very best florist. She sat down and stared at it for a moment, and then began carefully removing the wet newspaper from around the stems. 'How enchanting,' she said. 'What a darling your mother is.'

Jonathan got up abruptly. 'If you'll excuse me,' he said, 'I've got some papers to look through before tomorrow.'

'Oh, go ahead. *Please.* And oh, by the way, what time is that agent coming in the morning?'

'Nine o'clock.'

'I'll leave you to it then.'

'Right.'

'Good night.'

'Er – good night.'

She put the flowers in water and went to bed. It had been a long three days, and underneath her defiance she was suffering what she could expect to be a long-enduring and horrifying pain.

# 29

'Where have you been all this time?'

'I've been fetching Henrietta.'

'But you've been gone for ages.'

'Well I stayed for a drink with Louisa.'

'Yes, but still.'

'It's nice to be missed.'

'I couldn't find the whatsit.'

'Poor you.'

'You left here before tea-time.'

'Oh, yes, well, I popped in on Nicola.'

'*Nicola?* Why did you do that?'

'I'll explain later, I have to bathe Henrietta.'

'Why isn't Marie-Laure giving me my bath?'

'See if you can guess.'

'She's got a pain.'

'No.'

'She's lost.'

'No.'

'She's gone to her English class.'

'No, silly, not on Sunday. It's her day off.'

'When's she coming back?'

'After you've gone to bed.'

'I'm going to wait up for her.'

'No you're not. She'll be very late.'

'Fergus is allowed to stay up late. Fergus stays up till midnight, every night.'

'Oh, yes?'

'He does, he told me.'

'Good old Fergus. Come on, out you get.'

'Mummy.'

'Yes?'

'Why do I have to be good?'

'We all have to be good.'

'Why?'

'There is a reason, but I've forgotten it.'

'Merember it.'

'I'll try. Daddy will remember it – you can ask him. Now quick, nightie on. Dressing gown. Slippers. Good girl.'

Henrietta was eating her supper at the kitchen table.

'Daddy.'

'Yes?'

'Why do I have to be good?'

'Ask Mummy.'

'She's forgotten. She said to ask you.'

'Ah. Let me think. Ah, yes. Because . . .'

'Because why?'

'I don't buy icecreams for bad girls.'

Henrietta thought for a moment. 'When I grow up,' she said, 'I'm going to be bad, because then I'll have my own money, and I can buy my own icecream. I'm going to be bad, and buy my own icecream.'

'Well, that sounds reasonable enough,' said Alfred. 'But meanwhile, you'll have to be good, is that understood?'

'Alright,' said Henrietta reluctantly. 'But only until I grow up.'

Soon after this she went to bed, and Alfred read her some Winnie-the-Pooh, and she fell asleep just as Kanga . . .

# 30

'Why did you go to see Nicola?'

'Because she's sad.'

'Why?'

'Don't tell a soul. I probably shouldn't tell even you.'

'Fire ahead then.'

'Well—'

'Get on with it.'

'Jonathan's got cold feet.'

'What do you mean?'

'Bloody Jonathan has handed Nicola her cards.'

'He what?'

'He's offered to buy her out. The show's over. He's given her the elbow.'

'Was he there?'

'No, of course not. He delivered the blow and then more or less bashed off immediately to his parents for the weekend. She's hoping to bring him round, but it doesn't really look likely, does it?'

'Bloody Jonathan. How very unfortunate.'

'Yes, so say I.'

'I thought they were a permanent fixture.'

'Yes, naturally.'

'Awkward, isn't it?'

'Very.'

'I thought she was his salvation.'

'Perhaps he doesn't want to be saved.'

'Or he doesn't believe that she can save him.'

'Perhaps she can't, at that.'

'Who knows?'

'Only God; as usual. In any event, they won't be coming with us to the cottage at Easter, so I thought we might take Fergus.'

'Oh, God, must we?'

'Yes, Louisa's looking awfully peaky; she and Robert could probably use a break. Anyway, it's nice for Harry to have another kid to play with.'

'Alright, let's bite the bullet, then.'

So that was what they did.

# 31

Nicola lay under the bedclothes, hunched around her pain, despising herself.

She despised herself for her failure to oppose Jonathan's frozen blankness with the tears and shrieks which would have expressed her true feelings. She despised herself for the mean little sarcasms which had been her only mode of attack – she despised herself even though these slights had found their petty targets, because the wounded pride to which they gave expression was – or ought to be – the least of her complaints. She believed that the wound Jonathan had dealt to her heart (her truly loving, trusting, faithful heart) was a more serious and more honourable wound than that to her self-esteem. She supposed these two could be differentiated, and so long as they could, she had shown him nothing of the real pain she was suffering. In the face of his cast-iron indifference she was apparently as dumb and cold as he. She despised herself for this dumb coldness. She had never before so plainly been shown the difficulty, the near-impossibility, of speaking truly to an interlocutor who will not hear, but she knew one must attempt it nevertheless, and thus far she had failed even to make the attempt. She swore she would make it on the morrow, and at last, wretched, now, beyond tears, she slept.

She left the flat on Monday morning long before her usual time, and when she got to Fitzrovia, where she worked, she found an empty table in a coffee shop. She ordered a large filter coffee and a croissant. (Hugh would have been delighted: what had he told you? there!) She took a long time eating it and then she smoked a cigarette. She might do this every morning now. She was free to do exactly as she pleased, now, almost whenever it pleased her. She need never think of Jonathan at all. She was free, she was horribly, abominably free. Was this, in fact, what Jonathan himself wanted? This freedom, this horrible, this abominable freedom? She would, she swore, find out. She would see.

Jonathan did not return to the flat that evening until after nine o'clock. It could be supposed that he had eaten dinner somewhere else. Nicola was in the sitting room. 'Jonathan,' she called, hearing him enter. 'Could you come in here? I have to talk to you.' But she did not imagine that the irony was evident to him.

He stood, as had she, in the sitting-room doorway, looking not startled but tired and drawn. 'What is it?' he said. She got up. 'Come in,' she said. 'Sit down.' He entered the room with a terrible reluctance. 'Sit down,' she said again. 'Don't make this worse than it is.' He sat down. 'What do you want?' he said. 'The truth,' she replied. 'I've already told it you,' he said. He moved slightly as if to get up. 'The whole truth,' she said. 'All of it. I have to know.'

'This is useless. I *have* nothing more to tell you. I'm sorry, I wish I had. I wish I could satisfy your curiosity, but I can't. There is nothing more to know. I'll speak as plainly as I can. I'm sorry that you find this so hard to take in, but I don't want to live with you any longer. This relationship is getting us nowhere. I don't love you.'

She was silenced; she felt almost faint. He had said the words. Black silence surrounded her. She sat down: she *was* faint.

'I'm sorry,' he said. 'But that is the truth. You asked for it. Oh, by the way, that agent came – they'll send a written valuation, it should turn up in the next day or so. Then we can get cracking. Meanwhile, if you have no further questions, I'll leave you—I've got some work to look at.'

'Can you remember,' said Nicola, fighting for her life, 'when you last made love to me? Can you remember when that was?' He shrugged dismissively and pulled a face; the question was out of order, it was in poor taste. 'I can,' she went on. 'It was just a week ago. Last Monday night. Three nights before you told me to push off. Which means, that in only three days, just *three days*—'

'Oh, that,' said Jonathan. 'That means nothing. Sex. That's a quite separate matter. It means absolutely nothing. It has *nothing* to do with love.'

The thing to do—this at least she had grasped—was not to be deflected from the chief issue, not to be diverted by surprise or anger from the line she meant to and must pursue. 'You can't mean this,' she said. 'You can't possibly mean this.' He shrugged again, as if to say, have it your way; say what you like; I know what I mean. 'You must have forgotten everything,' she said. Her voice rose. 'That it had everything to do with love was always the whole point. You can't have forgotten, you *can't*.' Still he said nothing; he even turned his head away, impatient to be gone.

# 32

That sex had everything to do with love had always been the whole point. It had always been perfectly evident to Nicola that one could not have sexual intercourse with a person one did not seriously love: it was a physical and spiritual impossibility, and the more she witnessed of the readiness of other human beings to disprove this contention the more incredulous she grew, until she could only at last shrug and say to herself, so be it. Nicola could not even imagine how – physically, spiritually – one might so much as *take off all one's clothes* in front of – that is, for – a man (or, as the case might be, a woman) whom one did not truly, deeply, and with all one's heart know, and trust, and love. The imperative seemed to be physiological as much as it was moral. But as the years had gone by she had never managed to encounter anyone who truly shared these scruples. She had begun to think that there might be something significantly abnormal about her, physiologically or morally or spiritually, but she dressed up and went out when invited to do so none the less, hoping for enlightenment from one direction or another.

Two years ago she had gone in just such a mood of wary optimism to a rather rowdy party – she was getting just a little too old for this sort of thing – in Fulham. She was wearing a very short red skirt, and she had a red feather boa round her neck. Some time after midnight a heavy young man had stumbled or been pushed against a table in the kitchen and several glasses had crashed to the floor. Nicola had been getting herself a drink of water from the kitchen tap. She managed to herd the several people in the room out of it and back into the mêlée, and then she hunted down the dustpan and broom, and began to sweep up the broken glass. She had just crawled back out from under the kitchen table, dustpan in hand, when a voice from the doorway asked if she needed any help.

'Do you think you could try and find some newspaper?' she said, looking up at a rather tall, rather diffident-seeming, rather angelic-looking stranger. He entered the room gingerly, wary of the remaining broken glass, and began opening cupboards and peering into them. In due course he found a section of the previous week's *Sunday Times*, and helped her to wrap up the broken glass, which he deposited in the waste bin. Then he held out his hand to her. 'Jonathan Finch,' he said. 'Nicola,' she replied; 'Gatling.' 'Like the gun,' he said. 'Like the bird,' she replied. 'Yes, I suppose you get fed up,' he said. 'Everyone must say that.' 'Almost everyone,' she said. 'Are those gatling feathers?' he said, looking at the feather boa. She laughed. 'Can I get you a drink?' he said. 'I was just about to leave,' she replied. 'I never stay long after the first breakage.' 'I couldn't offer you a lift, could I?' he asked. 'I've only had one drink – I haven't been here long; I came on from the theatre.' 'Oh, you're a surgeon, are you?' she asked. 'Was it an emergency?' He looked astounded and then laughed. 'The West End theatre,' he said.

It was even less Jonathan's sort of party than it was Nicola's, but he'd been brought by the girl he'd taken to the theatre. He wouldn't have come, but there was a great hole in the middle of his life; he'd only just lately noticed it, and it was beginning to worry him. There was something he hadn't understood, or noticed, or reckoned on, and now that he was aware of the fact he was inclined to go wherever – within reason – fate suggested, hoping to find a clue. It was the most imaginative decision he'd made since his distant, so different, adolescence. And now, striking up this acquaintance with this girl in a red feather boa, moving in so fast: it was so entirely out of character – as previously delineated, since the beginning of maturity at all events – but there was your answer: he'd been right to come here after all.

'But did you come here by yourself?' she said. 'No, that's alright,' he replied. 'The girl I came with lives upstairs – I'll just say good-bye to her. She wasn't really expecting me to stay long. We're just – friends.' 'If she really won't mind,' said Nicola. 'If you're sure.' It wasn't the feather boa, it was, to begin with, her legs, and then, when she'd stood up, that rather grave little face. Well, it was, perhaps, the combination, of that red feather boa and that grave little face. He couldn't wait to get her away from all this noise and music and hectic activity.

# 33

He drove her, pretty fast, to Notting Hill and they chatted a little on the way; they discovered each other's occupations, but very little more. Nicola, glad simply to have been taken home without the trouble of finding a taxi, thanked him very much and went up to bed. A very nice-looking, possibly somewhat inhibited, probably rather dull chap whom I'll never see again, she thought, but it was awfully lucky he turned up like that.

In the middle of the week he telephoned her at work. So he'd been paying more than casual attention when quizzing her according to the usual polite formula: she was disconcerted. They met for a drink in a wine bar in Charlotte Street. Later that evening they found themselves dining together: it looked at if they might be getting on rather well. He was still very nice-looking – not to say, rather angelic – and might be somewhat inhibited, for all one knew, but it wouldn't be correct to call him dull.

Without the feathers, in her working clothes, she was still grave, still the sort of girl who'd sweep up the broken glass at a rowdy party before it caused a nasty accident: she had an edge of fastidiousness which was a challenge to him, and Jonathan was no stranger to challenge; a challenge was something he could respect.

After a few weeks he began to ask himself, wonderingly, if the feeling which seemed to be growing in him indicated that he was falling in love: because he hadn't heretofore believed that this was a thing one really did; he'd come to suppose that it was something done only by characters in fairy tales. They went on seeing each other; there were so many things to do – London was one immense cornucopia of inducements to be enthralled; even quite speechlessly to marvel. He'd never quite apprehended this before. The whole city was in actuality a great pleasure garden: it had obviously – but in secret – been designed expressly in order to entice its denizens into the silken bonds of love. Now he saw at last what everyone else had always, plainly, understood, that it was no mistake after all that Alfred Gilbert's famous statue at the very centre of the whole glittering maelstrom should have come to be known as Eros. The inconclusive, aborted infatuations he'd felt in the past for other women had been like the attempts of infant children to talk: what he felt now had brought him to the verge of true language. And yet, as the weeks went by, he did not speak.

Nicola began none the less to be sure that he would: Nicola had very quietly and distinctly apprehended that Jonathan was – very probably – the last remaining male of her own circumspect species. They were like those frail animals one sees in television documentaries: crowded out by other stronger and more successful competitors, they hunt for each other, trying (before it is too late) to mate. The ritual (they might be the very last of their species to perform it) continued over a period of some months, stage by delicate stage; at last they found themselves sweltering together in the heat of a black July night. They'd been to a concert on the South Bank, and now they were in Nicola's sitting room, drinking iced tea.

# 34

'Be quiet a moment. Listen. Can you hear that saxophone? There. Did you hear?'

'Yes. Nice.' They were silent again, listening. 'That's "Summertime", isn't it?'

'I believe you're right. Goodness, how corny.'

'No, it's nice. Do you think he's all alone?'

'It might be a she.'

'Women don't play the saxophone.'

'Are you quite sure about that?'

'Positive.'

'Let's go and look out the back and see if we can see him. Her.'

'It's probably a record.'

'No, it's solo.'

'It might still be a record.'

'Let's go and look.'

Nicola jumped up from the old rickety sofa and went into the bedroom and Jonathan followed. They leaned out of the window and saw only trees, thickly in leaf, and a light shining out on to the balcony of the first-floor flat in the next-door house.

'I think it's actually coming from there.'

They listened again. 'Summertime' ended, and the player paused for breath, or refreshment; the nearby darkness was silent except for a very faint stirring in the leaves.

'It's much cooler in here,' Nicola remarked. 'It would be, it faces north,' said Jonathan. 'Let's stay in here,' said Nicola, sitting down on the end of the bed. 'There might be more music in a minute.' Jonathan sat down near her. Nicola had not turned on the light when they had come in, so she said, 'Do you want the light on?' 'No,' said Jonathan. 'It's nice in the dark.' It was time, at last, to speak, and so, slowly, they began, at last, truly to speak. And there was not then, or later, any need ever actually to say: this is what it means to love you: this is what loving you means: and that there was no need was always an essential part of the whole point. Lovemaking was an esoteric language which they were now entirely qualified to speak. Even when the novelty – the marvel – of discovery wore off, this was a fact which Nicola at any rate simply and ineradicably knew.

# 35

'Jonathan,' she cried, now; 'don't − *don't* get up, don't go away. We have to finish now that we've started, we have to have this out.'

He turned his head towards her again and smiled very faintly, as one who, patient beyond all expectation, was prepared to humour her. 'But I've told you already,' he said, 'there's nothing to *have* out.'

'Very well,' she said. 'Very well. Very well, there may not be. You may not be the person I believed you to be. I have to know this. I have to know who you really are, who you really have been.'

'It makes no odds now, surely,' said Jonathan − still in the same tone of sweet reason. 'It does to me,' Nicola cried. 'I have to *know*, it will *kill* me not to know. Please,' she continued, trying desperately to control her voice, 'don't make this even worse than it already is. Can't you see what you have done to me? I loved you, I love you still: nothing that we've ever done together, *especially* our lovemaking, has ever had any other meaning for me. I thought you felt the same. I thought that was the whole point and now you tell me this. It's like being murdered.'

He was, at last, affected. 'I'm sorry,' he said quietly. 'If you really feel like that − yes, I can see that this is a shock for you. Of course, you're right. Of course, I was in love with you to begin with, and even for quite a time afterwards. Obviously, we wouldn't have set this household up together if we hadn't both felt like that. That's water under the bridge, unfortunately. I'm sorry about that too. Quite as sorry as you are, I dare say. But I suppose no one goes on being in love. It simply isn't humanly possible. I suppose the best one can hope for is that the state of being in love becomes a state of simply, well, loving. And unfortunately that hasn't happened to us. At least, not to me. I'm sorry, but there it is. I can't pretend, can I? You'd hardly want that. We've got to be realistic, and cut our losses.'

Nicola was feeling faint again with the horror of it all, but she knew this might be her only opportunity to discover what she could of the truth. 'When—' she said, 'when – did you stop caring about me? How long has it been, that you've just been going through the motions—' 'Oh,' said Jonathan, 'who can say? Several months, perhaps.' She felt ill, not only with the shock and pain that everything he had said had produced in her, but also with shame. She felt so horrifying and unthinkable a shame at the idea that Jonathan had even once, never mind many times, made love to her while feeling in fact no love, only this growing cold indifference, that she could almost have run from this place and hidden herself for ever. 'Christmastime,' she said, brokenly, remembering it, remembering the presents. 'Did you feel like this at Christmastime?' She remembered the white satin night-dress, and other matters.

Jonathan thought for a moment, remembering too. He pulled a face. 'No,' he said judiciously. 'I still loved you then. It must have changed after that. But look, please drop this cross-examination. I really don't remember the date. The only salient thing is that it's happened, that's all.'

'Supposing it happened straight after Christmas,' Nicola said, wonderingly, sick with shame and astonishment, 'you've gone on, all this time, three months or so, isn't it? as if – you've made love to me dozens, I don't know how many, times, as if—'

Jonathan's lovemaking, silent, intense, like a ritual enacted in a state of possession: she could begin to see that he might conceivably have continued to give the performance in a state of cold indifference: she saw now that, this being the case, she had actually been violated.

'Yes, well,' he interrupted her, 'since you insist on making such heavy weather of this, I might suggest that you're being rather naïve, aren't you? As you'd be the first to remind me in other circumstances, men are different from women in their attitude to sex if not in every other way as well. I mean, it's no big deal, Nicola. It doesn't mean anything. When it's there, you have it and when it isn't, you don't. Of course when one's in love it means more, I suppose, but that really is by the way. You're an attractive woman, obviously any man in my situation would have been glad enough to fuck you, it doesn't mean anything one way or the other. Alright, I grant you, it did once, but it doesn't now. It hasn't lately.'

'I see,' said Nicola. She had been not only violated but entirely destroyed.

'I admit,' Jonathan went on, in a brisk tone, 'it's rather second rate, but that's the whole point, isn't it? I mean, that's why I realised that it really was time to call *time*. Get on with our lives. And I suppose, now I come to think of it, that that business about your stopping the pill might have been a factor. I mean, I imagine you'd like to have a child or two some time soon, which means settling down in earnest, and I'm not your man for that. It simply wouldn't be fair to hang on as one's been doing, really it wouldn't. I'm sure you can wholly agree to that at least. So—'

'Yes,' said Nicola. She was so ill now with the horror of it all, and above all with the realisation, at last, that Jonathan had, indeed, meant what he had said, and had known what he meant, and that their relationship was now truly over, that she could say no more; she got up as one in a dream and went into the bedroom and shut the door.

# 36

'Bloody hell,' thought Jonathan. 'Bloody *hell.*' And he continued to sit there for a moment, staring at the empty grate and brooding. Then he got up abruptly and went to the doorway to retrieve the briefcase which he had left there upon first coming into the room. He sat down again and opened it and took out a thick folder of documents, and started to look through them, but after a short time he put them aside and stared once more at the empty grate.

It's her own bloody fault, he assured himself. She *would* insist on knowing. She wouldn't be put off, she *would* peer into my soul: if she doesn't like what she sees it's her own bloody fault. How utterly typical. First they insist on getting it out of you, and then they blame you for the resulting injuries. They'll never bloody learn. Still, just so long as she's got the message. Roll on, peace and quiet. And he picked up the folder again and began to look at the top document once more. It was only now that he suddenly noticed that he was still dressed for the office, so he got up impatiently and went to change. Returning to his work once more, he settled down properly at last and was soon absorbed in its intricacies.

Much later, glancing at his watch, he saw that it was nearly midnight: as late as that! He straightened up the papers and put them back in his briefcase, turned out the lamp and went to the room which was now no longer spare, but his; but as he did so, glancing at the fast shut door of the chief bedroom, his step faltered for a moment. He had not heard her move, or open the door – she was still, the woman who had pleaded with him and then quailed at his words, silent, even sequestered, within, behind that closed door. Was she asleep or awake? Was she alright? Well, it was none of his business, after all. She was a free agent now. The worst was over. She was a free agent, as was he. He could once more call his soul his own: as could she. End of chapter, end of story. And so to bed.

The evening's events, jumbled out of sequence, ran through his head again as he drifted and then slid towards sleep, until, in an anomalous instant, he suddenly seemed to see, flashing up at him, a ruby eye as of a phoenix. It flashed, staring at him, and then it vanished, and with it his last conscious apprehension of the elongated day.

# 37

The dark-haired young man behind the counter in the coffee shop seemed to half recognise her this morning: he nodded when she gave her order, identical to that of the previous day, as if to say, of course. He brought the coffee and the croissant and placed them before her with a sort of gentle deference, and with the same gentle deference – one step backwards before turning – withdrew.

Nicola saw all this as if through the wrong end of a telescope: the world beyond her seemed to have been miniaturised by the lens of her anguish. Once in the office she was forced to make a monstrous effort to bring this world beyond into something like normal focus, but it was always in danger of slipping back again, she always on the verge of losing control.

But she was lucky in her work: there was always too much – that is, enough – to be done; by mid-morning she and her word processor were enjoying something like their usual ambivalent relationship. She was drafting a section of a submission to the Arts Council, which would in due course be seen, marked and re-drafted by another greater hand before being re-written *in toto* and being given into a still greater hand for final comment and, it had to be hoped, approval.

She worked on: she had promised herself, early this morning, while she showered and very carefully dressed, that no one here should see the slightest sign of the horror which had befallen her. For she had indeed – she saw – been murdered. Jonathan's speech had ripped away a veil of delusion into which her very soul had been woven. If he had ceased to love her, if their conjunction had become meaningless, if she must now, as she must, now, leave him and their home, then she was no longer the Nicola she had known and unquestioningly been. No one at the office should know this: she should continue to play the part of Nicola and play it so impeccably that during the hours she spent here even she might suspend disbelief. It required only total concentration.

At lunch-time she sent out for a sandwich and worked on while the office slowly emptied around her. At last they were all gone. She carried on valiantly for a few minutes but then abandoned the machine, and pushing aside the half-eaten sandwich and the half-drunk coffee, and leaning her elbows on the desk, she buried her face in her hands, and sat thus, immobile, abandoned for a time to the unveiled acknowledgement of white-hot relentless pain. It will get better, she told herself at last, it must get better; I have only to live through this. She did not see that it would get better in some ways, and worse in others, would change its shape and colour through the days and weeks to come so as at all times to possess her mind and ensure her suffering until at last it was pleased to retreat. I must, she thought, just concentrate on what comes next, and try to live through this as decently as I can. She was not British for nothing.

# 38

'Susannah?'

'Oh, Nicola – at last! I was going to ring you myself—'

'Susannah, listen, I have to ask you a favour—'

'Are you going to come and stay here? Will you come tonight?'

'Are you quite sure you can bear it? I'm not much fun at the moment. I'm no fun at all, as a matter of fact.'

'You will be. Of course I can bear it – when will you come?'

'On Saturday – is that alright?'

'Yes, of course it is. Why do you keep asking? I think you should come today, tonight.'

'I can't, I have to sort my things out and so on. I'll come on Saturday.'

'Alright, Saturday. Are you alright?'

'No, I think I might have died and gone to hell, I'm not quite sure.'

'Oh, Nicola.'

'I'll be alright.'

'I think we should kill Jonathan. I think that might be best.'

'No, it won't make any difference.'

'It will make me feel better.'

'Oh, well, that's a good enough reason. Alright, kill him.'

'We'll plan it together after you get here.'

'I have to go now, Susannah, I have to go to the Tuesday meeting.'

'Oh, yes, that. Well, look—'

'I'll be with you on Saturday about mid-day, OK?'

'I could come and fetch you, shall I do that?'

'No, please don't worry, I'll get a taxi.'

'If you're sure.'

'Yes. Susannah—'

'Yes?'

'Thank you so much. *So* much.'

'Just take care, Nicola. We love you. Till Saturday!'

Susannah replaced the receiver and stared at the telephone. So it really had happened. Nicola had lost her lover and her home, just like that, *kaput*. What vile cruelty. It was like an Act of God in its suddenness, its comprehensiveness, its magnitude; it left one gasping. It was almost enough to make a person start smoking again: one really might as well, considering how many much worse ills awaited one. For several minutes the world looked to Susannah unutterably dreadful. Then she went on with her work. She was a picture researcher and at the moment she was attempting to collect together colour transparencies of all the paintings of J.-B. Chardin. She picked up one which had arrived in that morning's post and looked at it again through the viewer. The world was unutterably dreadful, *but*. There might be almost nothing one could do about it, but there was after all something one could do in spite of it. Hallelujah, she said to herself, hallelujah. Whatever that may mean. And so she consoled herself.

# 39

Jonathan had not come back to the flat on Tuesday night by the time Nicola went to bed, but the next morning she found signs of his having eaten a sketchy breakfast before vanishing again, still unseen. A sort of dull fatigue had taken possession of her but she too was reluctant to linger here: once more she left the house much earlier than usual and once more she went into the little coffee shop. 'Good morning,' said the young man politely. She managed to smile at him. 'Filter coffee?' he said. 'And one croissant?' 'Thank you,' she said, and she sat down at the same table as before.

When she returned to the flat that evening, after having worked on well past the usual time, there was a letter lying open on the kitchen table. Attached to it was a note: 'For your information, J.' It was the house agent's valuation. She put the letter back on the table and then on second thoughts found a pen and wrote at the bottom of Jonathan's note the single word 'Noted' and her initial.

Still Jonathan did not appear; Nicola returned to the task of sorting out her clothes and other possessions: those she must take away immediately, those she must leave behind to be called for in due course, those she would throw out. What else should one do, dazed by grief, but sort out one's possessions? Just before she fell asleep she thought she heard Jonathan coming in, but she was too exhausted to be dragged back from the brink, and if he made any further sound she was unconscious of it.

On the following morning she simply smiled at the young man in the coffee shop, and said, the usual, please, and he grinned back: right you are, he said; coming right up. As she sat down she at last saw why it was important, and even essential, that she should come here each morning, that she should continue to have this glancing encounter with this nameless dark-haired young man:·because it was the only one in which she was not known to be – to have been – the Nicola who had lived with Jonathan; loved Jonathan; belonged, altogether, to Jonathan. Here, and only here, she could fairly purport to be unashamed and whole. It might be a sort of rehearsal for a new existence.

By ten o'clock that night she had finished sorting out all her more personal belongings: these included the china dogs from the mantelpiece, which was now quite bare. She sat down on the sofa and looked at it, forcing herself to contemplate this detail of the enormity which had overtaken her. At last she heard Jonathan's key turning in the lock, and got up, and he, seeing the light, came unbidden to the doorway.

'I shall be leaving here on Saturday,' she told him quite calmly. 'I'm going to stay with Susannah for the time being. If you need to get in touch with me for any reason you can call me at the office. Or write to me.'

He seemed taken aback, and said nothing; she went on. 'I won't be able to remove everything on Saturday,' she said. 'Some of my things will have to wait until I've got my own place. If they're in your way, *tant pis*. Finding something else to do with them is one more thing than I can manage.

'As for the books, the tapes and CDs, the furniture and the etcetera – do what you like with them. I renounce all title. Oh, and there are a few boxes of stuff for Oxfam – perhaps you could drop them off some time if you wouldn't mind.'

He seemed by this stage of the speech to be stunned; he did not seem to know what to say. She shrugged. 'Well,' she said, 'I think that about covers it, so I'll leave you in peace.' She began to cross the room; but Jonathan stood, still, in the doorway, effectively obstructing her exit. 'Look,' he managed to say at last, 'there's no need, you know, to make a dash for it like this. I didn't expect—' but what was he saying? It was what he had in fact hoped for, as recently as last weekend: coming back from the country on Sunday night he had hoped, he had even expected, that he would find her gone. It was recent, but at the same time, how long ago that evening seemed! 'I didn't expect,' he repeated, 'that you'd be able to find somewhere else to live just like that, before we've even sorted out the money and so on – technically this is still as much your place as it is mine, after all. There's no need for you to camp out with Susannah.'

'No,' she said. 'Obviously you're right, *technically*. I'd simply rather.' 'Yes,' he said. 'I see.' 'And now if you'll excuse me,' said Nicola, 'I'm going to bed.' He stood aside for her and she left the room, and it was now that he saw what was different about it; *wrong* with it: the mantelpiece was bare; all the dogs were gone.

# 40

'Geoffrey, what have you done with the drill?'

'Why do you want the drill?'

'So that you can put up that rail.'

'What rail?'

'For Nicola's clothes.'

'Oh, not that again.'

'She'll be here on Saturday.'

'You're kidding.'

'I'm not though.'

'Oh, God.'

'So where's the drill?'

'Sam's got it.'

'*Sam?*'

'Yes, he borrowed it, a while ago, to put up shelves.'

'Honestly, you'd think with a whole house to fix up he'd buy his own drill. Pathetic.'

'Yes, well, there it is.'

'Well, you'd better get it back, pronto.'

'I can't go round there now, I simply *can't*.'

'You don't have to, Guy can go on his bike. Just ring up and say he's coming.'

'Oh, God, must I?'

'Please. I just want to get this bloody rail sorted out once and for all. *Now*. Look, I'll get the number for you. Where's that address book? Ah, here we are. Now.'

They did the business: Sam was in, thank goodness, because it was his turn to look after baby Chloe while her mother, the not-so-very-fair Helen, worked in an advice centre. Guy was called and sent off to do the errand and within half an hour Geoffrey with loud complaint was at work fixing the rail. The task itself was accomplished in ten minutes flat, it was only the stages leading up to it which had taken up a total of – conservatively – five hours, spread – to be fair – over four days.

'Shall I take it back to him now?' said Guy. 'He said he hadn't finished with it.'

'Of all the bloody cheek!' said Susannah. 'No you won't. He can bloody come and get it himself. The very idea!'

'How long is Nicola going to stay here?' asked Guy.

'I don't know. As long as she likes. Listen. I want you to be very very nice to Nicola when she's here, okay. Not that you wouldn't be, but still. She's feeling rather frail.'

'Frail. What does that mean?'

'Fragile.'

'Like glass?'

'Yes, exactly.'

'Might she break?'

'Yes. In a way.'

'Cor.'

'So just be very very nice, so that she doesn't.'

'I'll let her play with my mice.'

'That's the ticket.'

'She can have them in here if she likes.'

'That might be going a bit far. Just let her play with them, if she wants to. She might not want to.'

'Oh, she will.'

'We'll see.'

'Yes, we'll see – when's she coming?'

'Saturday.'

'Oh, but that's when I'll be at my riding lesson!'

'So, she'll be here when you get back.'

'Whizzy!'

# 41

She did not know where he might have gone, rising while she still slept and leaving the flat before she had got out of bed: bargain-hunting (some chance) in Portobello Road, or playing squash with some athletic crony, or simply wandering in a stupor of unease around the neighbourhood, up to the Gate, through the park, all the way to Kensington, and even beyond: who knew? He was returning, had already returned, to the secret state of his bachelor existence, before she had met him; all that was wanting was the murk of Crawford Street.

It was eleven o'clock already: she had done almost everything which had been listed under the rubric of 'last thing' and was anxious to be gone: to prolong the appalling horror of her departure – a horror so appalling that she could not face it, but had hidden from her grief behind a storm of activity – was out of the question. She would leave him a note. She began to write.

### Last Minute

1. Boxes marked Oxfam under window in bedroom.
2. 3 other boxes of my gear in wardrobe, to be called for a.s.a.p.
3. Don't forget to leave out wages for Mrs Brick on Weds. mornings – £20 (in cash).

She took the last load of laundry from the dryer and packed it and was ready to leave. First she would just take everything down to the entrance hall; then ring for a taxi. And that would be that. She put the front door on the latch and carried the first box downstairs.

As she was coming down with the second box she met Jonathan on the stairs.

'Oh!'

'I was just leaving.'

'Oh.'

'I'll be back for the suitcase in a minute.'

She continued on her way and then ascended the stairs once more and entered the flat. Jonathan was hovering in the sitting room. 'I'll just call a taxi,' she said; she picked up the receiver. 'I could take you,' Jonathan said. She glanced at him and began to telephone for the taxi; then she looked up again. 'Drop dead,' she said. Five minutes, the taxi controller told her. She hung up. 'I've left you a note,' she said, 'on the kitchen table. I wasn't sure you'd get back before I left. There's nothing more to say.' The telephone rang; she picked up the receiver and listened and after a word of thanks hung up. 'That's the taxi,' she said. 'Good-bye, Jonathan.' She walked over to the doorway and picked up the suitcase. 'Let me take that down for you,' he said. 'No,' she replied. 'I can manage it easily. Good-bye.' And she was out of the front door, and had closed it behind her, and was gone, just like that.

The driver helped her with the boxes and then they were off. She sat back in the rear of the taxi, looking at the gay and carefree Saturday crowds thronging the streets all the way across the Royal Borough, and then they were on the Albert Bridge crossing the mysterious Thames, and then they were in the otherworld of south-of-the-river, and Nicola, stricken almost unto death, sat there, immobile, incredulous, her broken heart thumping, thumping, her hands curled into fists so that she should not even begin to cry.

# 42

'Just go straight inside, darling – no one's there, Geoffrey's taken Guy to his riding lesson – I'll get the luggage.' Nicola went into the sitting room and sat down on the sofa and buried her face – down which as soon as Susannah had opened the front door her tears had started to stream – her terrible, strange, stricken face, in her crossed arms, and wept. Here were all the tears she had not shed during this terrible week: all the tears, for all the horror which had come upon her, and which, unendurable as it was, had to be none the less experienced. Then Susannah was with her. She cried for a very long time; Susannah had never heard a sound so utterly bereft. At last her tears subsided and she looked up, her expression hopeless and beaten. 'I think I might just pop over to Notting Hill and kill him now,' said Susannah matter-of-factly. 'Do you want to come with me, or would you rather wait here?' Nicola tried to smile. 'Hasn't Geoffrey taken the car?' she said.

'Oh, yes, I was forgetting. We'll have to wait until they get back. That won't be for another hour or so. They might stay out for lunch. Well, we'll have plenty of time to have a nice cup of tea first. And something to eat.'

'Just tea,' said Nicola. 'I can't eat anything.'

'Just a slice of ham? Nice ham from the bone? On a very thin slice of bread? With the tiniest dab of mustard? And just one *weeny* leaf of cress? Just to please me.'

Nicola managed to laugh, and then tears started coming out

of her eyes again. 'What would I do without you,' she said brokenly. 'You'd have to kill him by yourself,' said Susannah. 'Which might be quite difficult.' 'He's probably not even there,' said Nicola wanly. 'He's probably gone out.' 'I hope he gets run over then,' said Susannah. Nicola imagined the scene, Jonathan lying in the street, as still as death, covered in blood, and began to weep again in earnest. 'No,' she cried, 'don't say that! I don't want him to die!'

'Alright then,' said Susannah. 'Alright, alright. We'll let him live. But if he's going to live, he's going to have to shape up, he truly is.' And she began to wonder just how Jonathan might really have been living and thinking, and feeling, for the relationship to have come to this, and she thought it might be a good idea to do something about lunch, because then Nicola might be able to talk about everything which had happened, and she might gain some true perception of this extraordinary and terrible situation. 'It may be I who has to shape up,' said Nicola miserably. 'That remains to be seen,' said Susannah. 'The first thing to do is to have some tea and something to eat. Just a *tiny* snackette. Come on.' And she took Nicola's hand and they went into the kitchen.

# 43

So, she's gone, thought Jonathan, she has actually gone. It's all over; she's gone. And the flat itself seemed, from the moment that the front door had closed behind her, to have stopped breathing, to have been stilled into a silence so vacant that he was almost afraid to move, and still stood on the spot where he'd been standing, just inside the sitting-room doorway, when she'd made her exit, suitcase in hand.

But I should at least have helped her downstairs with her things, he thought. There had been something so disturbing about the sight of her, carrying that large cardboard box down the stairs, hardly able to see over the top of it. She could have missed her footing. She could have fallen down the stairs. She might have broken her neck. And then the suitcase. It must have been heavy. It's not as if she's an Amazon. That old 1950s pigskin suitcase, from her mother's old honeymoon luggage, with the watered silk lining beginning to fray: he remembered it, because they'd taken it on holiday to France last year, and it had earned them respect all over the Vaucluse. Useless for air travel, but just the thing on the road, in France. The French know how to read the signs at 40 paces, no, make that metres. One of the very best things about being English was living next door to the French, who among all their other talents knew how to *place* a piece of luggage at *quarante mètres*: you could roll up at a decent hotel dirty and tired and crumpled at the end of a long day, and they'd give you one of their looks, but as soon as they saw that suitcase it was *chouette*, it was *oui monsieur je vous en prie madame pas de problème. Voilà.* He could remember exactly how heavy that suitcase was, taking it out of the car, glad to hand it over to someone else to carry upstairs to their room, and now she'd taken it all the way down two flights of stairs by herself: I can manage it easily, she said. Well, it wasn't as if he hadn't offered. It wasn't his fault if he hadn't helped her. That he should have this sense of having left undone something he ought to have done was totally unreasonable. I suppose it's time I had something to eat, he thought, and then I can get on with some work: because he'd brought some work home for the weekend. This Lloyd's thing will go on and on *and on*, he thought: one of the biggest fuck-ups in the history of the world. It had come along at exactly the right moment for Jonathan: he was like an actor who has just been offered his first *Hamlet*. I'll just get something to eat. He was quite hungry now he came to think of it.

But he didn't go into the kitchen: instead he sat down for a moment on the sofa and looked at the fireplace, and wondered what was wrong, so terribly wrong; and then it came into focus again: it was the bare mantelpiece, of course. He remembered, now. She'd taken away all the dogs. Well, of course she had, they were her dogs. He hadn't even liked them all that much – he'd used to tease her about them at first; they weren't even good, most of them. 'Bad dogs,' he'd said. Except for the Derby pug he'd given her, that they'd seen one night, walking up Kensington Church Street together after seeing a film at the Odeon, looking in the windows of the antique shops on the way. 'Oh, look, Jonathan,' she'd said, in front of Stockspring, 'a little dog! Isn't it *sweet!*' He was happy enough to humour her. He looked at the dog indulgently. 'It is rather nice,' he said. 'A pug.' 'I expect it's expensive,' she said. 'Come on. But, oh, *sweet*. Look at its little face, and the tassels on its cushion.' 'Yes,' said Jonathan, making up his mind then and there; and he made a mental note of the telephone number on the fascia and rang the shop the very next morning, and got there just before they closed in the evening and bought the little dog, the dear little pug on its cushion, and took it home in his pocket, and when she was in the kitchen getting the casserole out of the oven, just before they sat down to eat at the dining table at the end of the sitting room – there, under the window – he'd put the little dog on her plate, and waited for her astonished, delighted, ecstatic discovery. The look on her face had been worth £300-odd of anyone's money.

And why, why on earth was he remembering all these things now? What point, what benefit, what pleasure, to him to remember such things now, or ever? It was just that, in this first hour or so of his new existence the flat was so extremely silent, felt so extremely empty, had ceased, so uncannily, to breathe. He might, after all, go out and get some lunch in a pub; yes, that would be best. He could do with a pint. Good. He got to his feet and checked his pockets to make sure he had plenty of money on him and left the flat, slamming the door to expel all the ghosts and goblins and wanly wandering spirits that threatened to take possession of its immensely yawning, silent emptiness.

# 44

'I hadn't done a proper shop for ages,' said Nicola. 'There can't be a scrap of food in the house.'

'You should worry.'

'All the same.'

'For God's *sake*. Sorry, sweetheart, don't want to be harsh, but I *mean*—'

'Oh, Susannah—' and Nicola began to cry again. Susannah patted her shoulder for a while, and poured her out a fresh cup of tea. Nicola dried her eyes. 'If only I knew,' she said miserably, 'what I'd done *wrong*.'

'Very likely, nothing *whatsoever*.'

Nicola was staring at the far wall in a terrible effort to see into the past, which can be more difficult even than seeing into the future. 'I suppose,' she said slowly, 'that it really was all brought on by my having to go off the pill.'

'The old pill has caused a lot of problems, one way or another, if you ask me,' said Susannah. Nicola, trying to laugh, managed to smile. 'I suppose that was what provoked Jonathan to consider the whole situation in depth, seriously,' she continued. She was smiling no longer. 'And then, to find it wanting. To find *me* wanting.' She paused. 'Which, after all, I am.'

'But not in his sense,' said Susannah sharply. 'He's the one who's wanting, in that sense. And if I know anything about it, he's going to end up wanting in the other sense too. He's going to be as miserable as hell, once he comes to his senses.'

'That's where he thinks he's come to *now*,' said Nicola. 'Well, he's entirely wrong there,' said Susannah very firmly. 'If you ask me, the poor sod's *actually* got a major rock in his head. So *there*.'

'I wish I *knew*,' said Nicola; 'I wish I really knew what it all *means*. The worst of all is not *knowing*.'

'Yes,' said Susannah, squeezing her hand, 'I know what you mean. That's always the worst. Nevertheless, *I* vote for the rock. Think about it.'

They were silent for a while, then 'Poor old Jonathan,' said Susannah, unexpectedly. Nicola looked at her, taken by surprise, and then briefly, faintly, smiled. 'Yes,' she said. 'I guess.' It was at this moment that, very fortunately, the front door opened and in a trice Guy came bouncing into the room. He leaped into the air and then struck an attitude. 'Shazam!' he cried. 'Shazam! Guess what?'

'Did you say hello to Nicola?'

'Hello, Nicola!' He turned back to his mother. 'Guess!'

'What?'

'I trotted today!'

'I say, well done! Whizzy!'

'You *bet*. I say, Nicola – Nicola, would you like to see my mice now?'

'I say, darling, I don't think—'

'I'll just go and get them – hang on a tick.'

'Oh, God. Sorry. He's been so looking forward to showing you his mice – can you bear it?'

'I've got nothing particular against mice.' In fact she loathed them, but fortunately Guy returned with just one, and she endured its running up her arm and sitting, terrified, on her shoulder, quivering. Then the sight of its fear and bewilderment aroused feelings of real pity, if not affection. 'Poor little thing,' she said. 'Poor little mouse.'

'She's not little, *for a mouse*,' Guy pointed out. 'She's quite big, actually, as a mouse.'

Nicola began to laugh, as did Susannah; in a while, Nicola was laughing almost helplessly, and Guy, pleased with himself, had joined in too. When Geoffrey came in he couldn't have seen even the slightest sign of anything but ease and merriment. Thank God at any rate for that, thought Susannah, with real gratitude.

# 45

The day died away around him, the dusk fell and the street lights came on; the liggers and the shoppers had all gone home and the revellers and rioters had not yet emerged: in the half-empty streets below him people walked their dogs and children circled each other on their bicycles, prolonging the last late evening minutes before going home to supper. Jonathan switched on the lamp and worked on for another hour.

Now it was dark; he got up and drew the curtains. Oh, but the silence! He turned on the wireless and went into the kitchen to see what he could find for dinner.

Now there was a thing. The food had been exclusively Nicola's department. They'd had an inequitable – if you like – arrangement whereby he paid all the quarterly bills and she paid for the food. Once a fortnight or so they went to Sainsbury's and stocked up, and she picked up other bits and pieces as and when and as Jonathan now discovered, opening the refrigerator, she hadn't been doing much picking up recently: why, after all, should she have? And he looked in the cupboards as well. Tinned soup, spaghetti, oil, vinegar, tea and coffee. Three eggs in the fridge, half a pound of butter, a hopelessly wilted lettuce and a sad tomato. In short, there was nothing to eat. There wasn't even any bread. He wasn't sure where he'd find a shop still open at this hour: the weekend catering, if not that of the lifetime ahead, was going to be an awfully big adventure. The only problem being, that he had no heart for it. Once more he checked his pockets to make sure he had enough money in them, once more he slammed the door upon the ghost-ridden flat, and went out into Notting Hill in search of sustenance. He chose the wrong direction, and so had to walk for a good ten minutes before he came to an open shop, but he managed to find everything he thought he wanted; two large carrier bags full. The place was full of people like him, lost souls shopping for groceries on a Saturday night. It was only when he got back to the flat and dumped the whole lot down on the kitchen table that at last he saw Nicola's note.

She'd left him a note – yes, he remembered, now. She'd told him she'd left him a note. He'd quite forgotten about it, what with one thing and another. What thing, and what other thing, could have made him forget? Here, waiting for him after that journey across Lethe, was Nicola's note: Nicola's last words to him before leaving. He did not want to read it – not yet. But he must. Yes, but first he would just open that bottle of Graves he'd noticed in the door of the refrigerator. Always keep a bottle of white wine chilled and handy: there are moments when you need a *petit coup de blanc* like nothing else. Corkscrew, glass, draw the cork, so. Pour. Sniff. Taste. Smoke, raspberries, potash, whatever. Hunter Valley, eat your heart out. Another *petit coup*. Right; now for Nicola's note.

### Last Minute

1. Boxes marked Oxfam under window in bedroom.
2. 3 other boxes of my gear in wardrobe, to be called for a.s.a.p.
3. Don't forget to leave out wages for Mrs Brick on Weds. mornings – £20 (in cash).

*I've left you a note,* she'd said. *There's nothing more to say.* No, quite:

how could there be? It was commendably succinct. There was not, there had not been, another word to say.

# 46

'How's Nicola then?'

'You *saw* how she was.'

'She seems perfectly okay to me, I don't know why you've been making such a song and dance. Rails, and God knows what else.'

'For Heaven's sake. Are you totally insensitive, or what? She's putting on a brave face. A *very* brave face. She's grief-stricken, that's how she *actually* is.'

'Are you serious, or are you serious?'

'Right both times. Seriously, she is completely grief-stricken. She has her episodes of calm and lucidity, but then – she just caves in. She's suffering from shock, clinical shock. It actually *is* a sort of bereavement.'

'Oh.'

'So just watch it, okay? Be gentle.'

'I'm always gentle.'

'And watch what you say.'

'All this for that wimp Jonathan.'

'She really loves him, you see. She really does. She gave him her heart and he broke it.'

'It's pure Country and Western. I might write a song, make us all rich. She gave him her heart and he broke it. I like it. Guy can have a horse. Whizzy!'

'Just so long as you don't *dare* try it out in front of Nicola. Remember what I said. Okay?'

'Yeah, yeah, sure. Look, that's enough Nicola for one day, okay? Could you hit that light? I'm falling . . . a . . . sleep . . . it's been a long, long . . . day . . .'

And tomorrow will probably be just as long, thought Susannah in the darkness. Bloody Jonathan. Miserable sod.

Nicola, too, lying in her strange bed in Susannah's workroom – at the top of the house, overlooking the back garden – was thinking of Jonathan. No amount of solitary thought, no amount of discussion with Susannah, however apparently reasonable their conclusions, exhausted the subject. Nicola was haunted by the suspicion that there was something she had not seen or even imagined; that there was something dreadfully wrong which had escaped her perception entirely: and yet no amount of thought or discussion might ever discover it. But this night as every night, as many times during the day, she once more entered the maze of remembrance in the hope of finding, this time, the path to the beast which might lurk at its heart. Perhaps Susannah was right in saying that there was a rock in Jonathan's head: but was it not possible, wondered Nicola, that the rock was in her own head? and that Jonathan, seeing or sensing its presence, had been right to say to himself, I don't actually love her; let's make an end of it.

But that being so, she wished – how she wished – that there had been some other way of doing so. The cruelty of his cold indifference had lacerated her. It was something she would remember with horror and shame all her days. It almost convinced her that it was indeed she who was at fault, and the worst of it all was that she could not see how, or where, or why. It was after three o'clock before she finally slept. So passed her first night away from the home whose loss compounded the grief which was engulfing her whole self.

# 47

It was a blustery, uncertain sort of day, with rushing clouds which seemed on the point of foregathering and darkening only to scatter again and admit the sunshine: one could not decide whether to go out or if so how far. 'We'll just go for a quick run on the Common,' said Susannah, 'okay?' Nicola was drying up the luncheon things and said nothing. She would do whatever was decided. She did not want to be awkward. Guy began to offer other more ambitious not to say altogether unrealistic suggestions; the doorbell rang. 'I'll go,' said Nicola unexpectedly. Susannah, eyebrows raised, threw Geoffrey a meaningful look: what had she told him?

Nicola opened the door. Before her was a short rather plump rather ginger-haired and bearded man with a baby in a pushchair. He gave her a startled look. 'Oh!' he said. 'Geoffrey not in? Or Susannah?' On being assured that they were he came in, pushing the baby before him, without further ceremony, Nicola (her heart thumping with a terrible disappointment) returning to the kitchen to summon her hosts. Out they came. 'Oh, Sam,' they said. 'Nicola, this is Sam. And this is little Chloe. Hello, Chloe. Come into the sitting room, Sam.' The sitting room – knocked through – occupied virtually all of the ground floor, the kitchen having been thrown out at the rear. Sam wheeled the baby into a corner and put on the brake and they all sat down. 'Will you have some coffee?' said Susannah. 'I was just about to make some. We've only just finished lunch.' 'I don't mind if I do,' said Sam. 'As long as you're making it anyway.' He looked around the room, especially at the pictures hanging on the walls, with a frankly speculative glance, as if checking to see whether anything new and/or valuable had come into it since his last visit. 'Still got that Hodgkin, I see,' he remarked. He often said this, as if to say, you must be doing alright, if you can afford *not to sell* a Hodgkin.

Geoffrey played up to this with gusto. 'Yep,' he said, with an air of oleaginous self-satisfaction. 'Still got it!' He all but smacked his lips. It was a very small Hodgkin and they'd bought it with a windfall about a million years ago, before acquiring a mortgage and a child and all that pertains thereto, but Sam didn't take any of that into account.

'Saw a very tasty little Sutton the other day,' he said. 'Couldn't afford it, of course.' He gave a sort of snort which implied better than any words could do not only the utter unlikelihood that such as he might afford such a thing but also the evident turpitude of anyone who could. 'Ah,' said Geoffrey cheerfully, to all appearances oblivious of these implications, 'a Sutton; yes. We haven't got a Sutton.' As if by mere oversight: a gap yet to be filled in a catholic – yet serious – collection. 'How much were they asking?' 'Oh, you know,' said Sam glumly, 'five figures. More than that I'm not prepared to say.' If I can't have it, he seemed to imply, I'll be damned if you shall. I won't even tell you where it is, so there. 'Cork Street, was it?' said Geoffrey innocently. 'Who *is* his dealer these days?' As if he genuinely required to know. 'Frankly, I don't exactly remember,' said Sam, almost ill-temperedly. 'One of those rascals, does it matter which?' He had Geoffrey there; he looked around the room again as if to change the subject. 'That chair's new, isn't it?' he said, almost accusingly. 'Not really,' said Geoffrey, all consolation. 'Only new to this room. We had it upstairs.' 'Oh, yes?' said Sam, as if to say, that's the rich for you: chairs all over the place; upstairs *and* downstairs. 'Nice, though, isn't it?' said Geoffrey urbanely. 'Arts and Crafts. We managed to get in early there. Couldn't afford it now, of course.' 'No,' said Sam abruptly. 'I should think *not*.'

Susannah had returned with the coffee half way through all this and had been throwing warning looks at Geoffrey, who had been ignoring them. She now seized her opportunity. 'How do you like it?' she asked her guest, having seen to Nicola already. 'Milk? Sugar?' 'Yes,' said Sam. 'Please. The lot.' Take them for all they've got. The funniest part of all, as Susannah and Geoffrey later explained to Nicola, who had taken in all these proceedings with wide-eyed wonder, was that Sam, being a colleague of Geoffrey's, was on exactly the same salary scale; although of course it was possible that Helen earned less than Susannah. It was also of course possible that she earned more. But there was little enough in it: in plain fact, Sam and Helen were as rich as they, and they as poor as Sam and Helen.

Guy, perhaps infected by Sam's need to be plied with all the luxuries of this world, perhaps on his own account, now enquired whether they might not now have a chocolate and was given leave to fetch the box, with which he returned at approximately the speed of light. Nicola having refused one they were offered to Sam. 'Hmmm,' he said, as if to say, chocolates, too. His hand hovered over the contents, and he chose one. He raised it nearly to eye level before eating it, as if to determine its provenance, and then it vanished into his mouth. 'I say!' he exclaimed. 'This chocolate is the business alright!' His frank delight made up for almost all his former malice: Susannah all but forgave him while Geoffrey having so revelled in the game had nothing to forgive. 'Yes,' said Susannah. 'They're a present from Nicola. Fortnum's, you see. Brilliant, aren't they?' She stopped herself just in time from observing that you get what you pay for. 'Have another,' she said. 'Alright,' said Sam. 'Just one.'

The disregarded baby now let out a yell. 'Oh, she wants one

too!' cried the heretofore silent and wondering Nicola. 'No,' said Sam abruptly. 'She can't. They're too rich for her, she'll be sick.' The baby began to wail. 'Just a tiny bit, then,' said Nicola. 'I'll give her a tiny bit out of mine.' She took the smallest one she could see, actually a chocolate-covered almond, and bit off a piece of the chocolate which she gave to the baby, who instantly ceased her clamour and smiled and waved her arms joyfully. Then she began to look around, as if for more; her smile faded and she began tentatively to wail anew. 'She'll never shut up now,' said Sam crossly. 'I was hoping she'd doze off while I'm here.' That was his social life down the tubes for the afternoon. 'Would you like me to take her out?' said Nicola. 'I could take her out for a walk if you like.'

This offer surprised them all, especially Sam. He had so far paid Nicola no attention whatever, although she was in fact the only new and valuable item in the room since his last visit. He turned his head and looked at her, genuinely astounded. 'Well,' he said. 'If you like. Yes, if you like. Yes, that would be very nice. If you're sure you can manage her.' You'd have thought she was a Doberman.

'Yes, we'll manage,' said Nicola. 'I'll just get my jacket.' The baby had stopped her tentative wailing and was listening with interest to this exchange, and she now kicked her legs in evident approval of the conclusion it had reached. When Nicola returned and began to wheel the pushchair out of the room she waved her arms joyfully again and uttered several small shrieks of happiness, and the two left the house.

# 48

'I wonder what has happened on the Jonathan and Nicola front.'

'What front? Where?'

'I told you. He's given her the push. Or he had when last heard from. Or rather, of. I was just wondering if they've managed to patch it up.'

'Oh, I expect so. He can't afford to screw up at his age. Got to settle down sooner or later, make a few copies of the old DNA before the packaging passes its use-by date, it's what we're here for.'

'Oh, that's funny, I thought we were here to pursue goodness, truth and beauty.'

'No, no, that's just an optional extra, it's only the DNA thingy which is obligatory. Time Jonathan got on with it.'

'Perhaps he just doesn't want to.'

'Well it's not really any of our business. Speaking of which—' Alfred put down his coffee cup and moved slightly closer to Lizzie, 'I don't suppose you've given any more thought to the matter of a sibling for Henrietta, have you?' He was looking rather sad. Lizzie put her head on his shoulder. 'It's awfully difficult,' she said, 'to find the time. You must understand.' 'Yes, yes, I know that,' said Alfred. 'But it always will be. And eventually it will be too late altogether.' He looked even sadder. 'I'm sorry, Alf,' said Lizzie. 'I really can't think of doing it now. This is a really crucial time for indies. Perhaps in about six months. That's the best I can say right now.' 'Okay,' said Alfred, still sad, but resigned, 'Okay. What can I say?'

'Look on the bright side,' said Lizzie.

'Which is that?'

'You know what a child can do to a marriage. I mean, we are happy as we are, wouldn't you say?'

'Of course I would. I wouldn't want us to have another sprog otherwise.'

'Yes, but what if another sprog were to ruin everything? It wouldn't be worth the price, then.'

'No, of course not, but why on earth should it?'

'Well, it can happen. Look at the Maclises.'

'Oh. Them. Well, but—'

'They were perfectly okay until they had Percy, and by the time he was walking it was all down the tubes. Awful. Poor Claire.'

'Well, poor Alex if it comes to that. He rang me the other day by the way; he wants to ply me with strong drink and pick my brains, he's doing a big piece about the Lloyd's thing.'

'Are you going to oblige him?'

'I dare say I shall, I'm an obliging sort of chap as you know.'

'Obligation, it's an interesting idea, isn't it? It's so very human. I'm sure animals have no sense of obligation. Which reminds me, I think I'm obliged to telephone Nicola and see if everything is alright, considering how upset she was when I saw her.'

'Oh, do it then if you must and get it over with.'

'Yes, but I'm afraid of getting Jonathan, which would be awkward, because he presumably doesn't know that I know, and I couldn't tell him that I did, and I have nothing else to say to him; it's Nicola I really need to speak to.'

'If she doesn't answer just say sorry wrong number and hang up.'

'You've done this before, haven't you?'

'Once or twice. In my rash and turbulent youth.'

'I think the best thing is to wait and ring her at work.'

'Yes, alright, you do that then.'

But naturally, what with one thing and another, this being, truly, a crucial time for independent telly producers, she forgot to—not that it mattered at all seriously.

# 49

'Will she be able to manage?' asked Sam, typically inspecting the bolt on the stable door with the horse already a good three fields away. 'Probably,' Geoffrey assured him; 'very probably.' 'Of course she will,' said Susannah hastily. 'She's got nieces and nephews, she's very experienced; she even used to look after Guy sometimes. Guy, perhaps it might be a good idea if you were to ride after them on the bike and make sure Nicola knows how to get to the Common in case she wants to go there. And we need some milk, so you might get that for me, would you?' 'Oh, alright,' said Guy without much enthusiasm. 'Thank you, darling,' said his mother. He sloped off and a moment afterwards they heard him leaving.

'Obliging sort of kid you've got there,' said Sam. Was there no end to their privileges? Geoffrey pulled his face into an expression of judiciousness. 'Yes,' he said. 'We feel, that – instil the aesthetic sense, and everything else will take care of itself. It seems to have worked, so far.' He paused and then turned to his wife. 'Wouldn't you say, Susannah?'

She ignored him and turned to Sam. 'How are things round at Cardamon Road? How is Helen?'

'Oh, as far as Helen is concerned, she is the reason for my bringing Chloe here. Can you take that child out for a walk, she said to me, I need some space. Space! In a house with six-plus rooms, she needs space!' 'I suppose she meant time,' said Susannah. 'How is the house?' At least I got out of that pretty quickly, she thought. Sam had been looking oppressed; but his expression did not now brighten. Oh dear, now what, thought Susannah: out, but not far enough out. 'That house,' said Sam heavily, 'is my Waterloo.'

The association at this juncture of Sam with Napoleon was unspeakably ludicrous; Geoffrey and Susannah both began to laugh helplessly. After one very disconcerted moment Sam himself began to join them and was soon laughing as heartily as they.

Having (however inadvertently) picked up the ball he now ran with it, treating them to a wild catalogue of mishap and disaster such as only a *bricoleur* can provide. Tears veritably pouring down their faces, they begged for respite, but he showed no mercy, and continued to sit, now glum-faced and hopeless, piling Pelion upon Ossa. 'And with all that,' he concluded at last, 'I still haven't managed even to touch the top floor. *Status quo ante*, right down to the kitchen sink. That top front room was meant to be Chloe's bedroom, with a study for me at the back, much as you've got here; but as it is she's right next door to us. No wonder our sex life has hit the buffers. Not that it wouldn't have done anyway, but every little helps.' 'Still, the kitchen must be looking pretty good,' said Susannah quickly. 'Ha!' Sam ejaculated mirthlessly. 'It's the charnel house of all my good intentions and all my fundamental optimism. If that's the sort of thing you go in for, it looks bloody good. Other than that, I could choke on it.' And he fixed them with a belligerent glare, as if defying them – or anyone else – to provoke him into doing so.

His hosts began to laugh again and were soon almost as helpless as before. 'Lastly,' said Sam, 'in any case, to look on the bright side, I'm going to have to pull in my horns for a bit—' Horns! It was too much, tears came into their eyes again; Sam looked from one to the other in blank astonishment and finding no ready explanation for their renewed mirth continued:' – because we've run into a cash-flow fuck-up, don't ask me how. But I really don't know which is worse, carrying on as I've been doing in the futile hope of finishing, some day, or stopping the show *pro tem.* If there's one thing I know about doing it yourself, it's that it costs a bloody fortune. In fact we're thinking of letting the top floor to some student or other desperate character. With that back room still fitted up as a kitchen, of sorts, they wouldn't be too much in the way, they'd only have to share the bathroom. That's what we'll probably do, after Easter.'

'Oh, yes,' said Susannah. 'Easter. Are you going away?' 'If you can call going to my parents *going away*,' said Sam. 'It doesn't fulfil any of the essential conditions except for the tiresome ones. Still, we'll be shot of Chloe, in the main. She'll be taken over lock, stock and barrel. That's something. Too bad we can't just send her by herself, to be collected at the other end like any other livestock, but BR won't wear it. No wonder they've gone to the wall. They won't provide the services the punters really need. So we've got to take her ourselves and hang about until it's time to bring her back again.'

'Where do they live, again?' asked Susannah. 'Cornwall,' said Sam morosely. You'd have thought the name designated one of the kingdom's most notorious hell-holes. 'Sounds lovely,' said Susannah firmly. 'Oh, it's lovely enough,' said Sam, as if loveliness were the merest and most paltry of attributes. 'What more could one ask?' said Geoffrey rhetorically. 'Ah,' said Sam. 'If I only knew.' Meanwhile, as they all immediately, perfectly, understood, he was asking anyway. The crystalline moment was shattered by the front door bell. 'That will be Nicola,' said Susannah. 'And with any luck, Chloe too,' added Geoffrey. 'I'll just go and see.'

'I suppose she'll be sopping wet,' said Sam lugubriously. 'That baby should be hooked up directly to Thames Water, I swear.

Then the rest of us might get a bit of peace.' 'The duck,' said Susannah fondly. 'The little precious.' 'Ha!' said Sam. *'So you say.'*

# 50

Sam had gone home with the baby and the electric drill, the retrieval of which had been his purpose in making the visit, and Nicola was looking at the job advertisements in the previous day's *Guardian*.

She often did this – supremely pointless as it was: for as was well known, no one ever actually got these jobs; no one was ever so much as short-listed; the entire exercise appeared in fact to be a sort of art form. Once in a while one might participate in it more fully by sending in an application, but it was essential in such an event to maintain the Dadaist stance.

'Scunthorpe Literary Festival,' she read; 'Assistant to the Director.' Just so. That sort of thing: her qualifications met the case exactly; there was not the slightest chance of her being considered. It was a six-month contract and the starting date was the first of June. She counted on her fingers. In and out before winter set in. It was perfect.

'Wouldn't you rather have a Sunday?'

'No, it's alright, I'd just as soon look at this. I missed it yesterday.' Scunthorpe: it seemed the ideal way of fleeing the chaos of heartrending anguish and struggle into which her life had collapsed. 'I think I'll apply for this job in Scunthorpe,' she said.

'Oh, but you can't possibly.'

'I think I will though. Don't worry, I won't get it.'

'So why bother applying?'

'Someone should.'

'Why you?'

'I just fancy it.'

'Well, so long as you don't actually get it.'

'No, I couldn't conceivably *get* it.'

Susannah had been studying the face of her friend. A notable alteration (it was too soon to say whether it was certainly for the better) appeared to have taken place in the last few hours: could one begin perhaps to hope for an early recovery? 'Guy will be out visiting his friend for the rest of the afternoon,' she said. 'So we were thinking that we might go and see a truly adult flick. Do you feel like doing that?' 'Which flick?' asked Nicola.

'See if you can guess.'

'Where's it on?'

'The NFT.'

'*Les Enfants du Paradis.*'

'No.'

'I give up.'

'Just one more.'

'Oh . . . *Singin' in the Rain.*'

'No! it's the *other* one.'

'I can't. You don't mean *The Red Shoes*?'

'No, no. The *other* other one. *All About Eve.* Wanna come?'

Nicola sat up. 'Just try and stop me!' she cried. 'Well, we should push off fairly sharpish,' said Susannah. 'It starts at five. I'll just go and round up Geoff.' She went upstairs; he was writing something on her word processor.

'I think our Nicola could be having a miracle recovery,' she said. 'Good,' said Geoffrey. 'We're going to see that film at the NFT, we have to leave soon.' 'Okay.' 'I wish you'd be more surprised at her recovery,' said Susannah. 'But I'm not surprised at all. I mean, a day or two with me – she can see exactly how wimpy and unworthy that Jonathan actually is. It stands to reason.' 'So it does. I was forgetting. Well, you can pay for our tickets then. That will put the lid on it.' And he did. But it didn't. Not that they knew this. There were things which not even Susannah knew. There were things which not even Nicola knew, or knew that she knew. One knows, after all, virtually nothing.

# 51

On the way home (seatbelts well fastened) they collected Guy and some Indian take-aways, and while they were eating Susannah brought up the subject of Easter, which fell the following weekend. 'Did you have anything planned,' she asked Nicola carefully, 'or could you come away with us? There's plenty of room.' This was rather an exaggeration, but it did not signify, because Nicola replied that she meant to visit her parents for a few days. 'I have to explain everything,' she said. 'I can't do it on the telephone.' She began to look distressed and Susannah searched for a way to carry the conversation forward.

'But the rest of the time,' she said; 'will you be alright here by yourself? We'll be away from Good Friday until the Saturday week. I don't want you to be lonely.' 'No, I'll be fine,' said Nicola firmly. 'I'll be just fine.' She dreaded it unspeakably. 'You could come to us after Sussex,' urged Susannah. 'I can't, I have to be back at work.' 'I was forgetting,' said Susannah. 'I'll be fine,' said Nicola again.

'We'll get Sam and Helen to keep an eye on you,' said Geoffrey. 'After they get back from Cornwall, at any rate. How would that be?' They all began to laugh, and then Susannah and Geoffrey told Nicola some of the bits she had missed while she was out with Chloe, and other things about Sam and Helen, and then Susannah remembered what Sam had said about his cash-flow problem. 'There may be a little pied-à-terre in the offing round there,' she said; 'I don't know whether you'd be interested.' She said it more as a joke than not. Nicola stopped eating and looked up at her. 'How do you mean?' she said. Susannah explained.

'When they first bought it the house was all divided into bed-sits, and they haven't got around to dismantling the top-floor one yet. There's a front room, like Guy's bedroom here, and the back room is a kitchen. I haven't actually seen it but Geoffrey has.'

'It's foul,' said Geoffrey. 'You'd loathe it. It's quite out of the question.'

'It would do for the time being though,' said Nicola. 'I need a bolt hole.' 'Oh, but you've got one!' cried Susannah. 'You've got a lovely bolt hole right here. We've put up a rail, and everything, and Guy's let you play with his mice – how can you even think of moving into another?'

'She can take the mice with her, if she likes,' said Guy. 'I don't mind.' 'You're all so very kind,' said Nicola. 'But I couldn't dare risk outstaying my welcome. Anyway this is rather premature, they may not want to let it to me.' 'You needn't worry about that,' said Geoffrey. 'If Sam wants to have my drill on an indefinite loan he'll have to do what I say. So if you want that space, just say the word, and I'll fix it for you, no problem.' 'But you just said it was horrible,' said Susannah. 'The best thing would be for me to see it,' said Nicola. 'And then decide.' Susannah looked doubtful and disconcerted. 'Well,' she said. 'I could ring Helen in the morning and suss it out. Then we'll take it from there.' 'Thank you,' said Nicola.

This was how she and Susannah and Guy (he having insisted) all came to be trekking up Sam's stairs the following evening after Nicola got back from work, to inspect the bolt hole. It was just as Geoffrey had described, but it was felt that when it had been cleaned thoroughly and given a coat of white emulsion it would be quite tolerable. Once Helen had grasped that Nicola would not be averse to minding Chloe occasionally in the evenings, she had no further questions or reservations, but urged Nicola to move in that very minute. It was none the less agreed that she would do so after Susannah and Geoffrey returned from their Easter holiday, in just under a fortnight's time.

# 52

The spare room was tiny, hardly more than a box room, but Jonathan had thought he might as well go on sleeping in it, now that his things were there. There did not seem to be any point in going to the trouble of moving them all back into the main bedroom again. The only real problem now was his shirts, the washing, drying and ironing of; it was real and it was even urgent, and he was going to get up and begin to deal with it this very minute.

For the rest, now that there was no one peering into his soul, he couldn't quite locate it. It seemed to have floated away somewhere just beyond his apprehension. Now it was he who was doing the peering, trying to find his soul, so that he could finally assure himself (for a strange and irrational doubt seemed to clutch at him) that what he had decided and what he had done were right. He knew he was right, but he did not feel right, and what was the use of being right if one were to be left feeling wrong? Feeling right seemed the better part of being right. But it's perfectly useless to lie here thinking, thought Jonathan; the thing to do is to get up and deal with my shirts.

He managed to get the washing machine loaded and switched on; now for some breakfast, he thought. So he got that started; as it was Sunday there was all the time one liked to take, one could make real coffee, even heat the milk. Plenty of toast. Something to put on the toast: he opened the cupboard to see if there might be some honey, or perhaps some strawberry jam, and he saw the marmalade.

Marmalade, said the handwritten label; and then the month and the year. They always did that, put the date. It was an ancient practice deriving from an era when this information was pertinent or even essential; a primitive form of the best-before date: quite pointless now. But they still did it. It was like the jam-making itself, an emblematic gesture: quite pointless now, in this age of intercontinental industrial jam production. Of course they said that home-made jam tasted better. Did it?

It was a large jar, one of those 2lb jobs; the contents were a rich tawny shade, almost brown. There wasn't, that he knew of, a name for this colour, but looking at it one could imagine how it would taste, and he realised that it was exactly what he wanted to eat. He almost craved it, he could all but taste it now. Marmalade. *But you used to love marmalade, I used to send it to you at school.* He remembered, now; he remembered eating it straight from the jar. It was angels' food. It was emblematic food. It was true that the commercial variety did not taste even remotely the same; it failed to achieve the balance between bitter and sweet which was the essence of the thing. Yes, marmalade: marmalade, yes.

Marmalade, no. This marmalade belonged to Nicola. *I must remember to take it with me when I go.* She had forgotten it. He could put it with her other things in the bedroom, for her to collect a.s.a.p. Not now, later. Later, later. The toast will be cold. It doesn't matter. He found some gooseberry jam and sat down.

Sunday breakfast in the empty, silent flat: senior back-benchers are reported . . . his soul was there, where it always had been, at the unlocated interface between brain and mind; it had come home – or he had – just like Mary's little lamb. That was Nicola's marmalade, and they were not now in a shared-marmalade situation. He knew he'd been right in principle, in essence: it was just the mundane details which took a bit of getting used to. Too bad about the marmalade. The balance between bitter and sweet was the essence of the thing.

# 53

It was Tuesday morning and Nicola was in the coffee shop eating a croissant, thinking hopelessly of the things still to be done. It got harder, not easier, as time went by: because as the shock wore off, the pain seemed to increase. There were moments when the pain seemed altogether insupportable: could one really survive such an experience?

There were things still to be done which she could not face: they could be done only at the eleventh hour: you knew that had arrived only when it seized you with its ice-cold claw. She still had for example to ask the Post Office to re-direct her mail: this was just beyond her present capacities, for she was not altogether certain where she was actually living, or for how long. She had after some thought sent the Scunthorpe application as from the Notting Hill address, since until the sale was effected this seemed to her to be her official residence; meanwhile, the thought of informing her other friends of the change in her circumstances was one more thing to be dreaded, and deferred. She needed all her resolution for the things which must be done immediately – the Scunthorpe business having been a diversion, feasible because so entirely unnecessary, not to say frivolous. Realising this, she all but smiled, and looking at the clock on the wall to make sure she had enough time still in hand lit a cigarette. At this moment a voice broke startlingly into her reverie.

'Nicola! Now what could you be up to, lurking in here like a wan swan?'

She looked up and saw Philip Colebrook, graphic designer –
in his own formulation – *extraordinaire*. He was the nearest thing
among her colleagues to a boon companion; someone to gossip
with, someone to giggle with; she smiled at him. 'Won't you
join me?' she said.

He sat down. 'I've never caught you in here before,' said Philip.
'I should have known someone else would find out my secret
cubbyhole, and that it would be you.'

'I won't tell anyone else.'

'Please don't. Why are you wearing dark glasses?'

'To hide behind.'

'What are you hiding from?'

'Myself.'

Philip missed a beat. 'How's that lawyer type,' he said, 'what
you're shacked up with? He hasn't given you a black eye, has he?'

'No, not a black eye. A bloody nose.'

Philip looked shocked. 'You don't mean—' he said; Nicola
put out her cigarette. 'We have to go on deck,' she said. 'Look at
the time. He's given me the elbow. *C'est fini. On est parti.* I'm
now living in Clapham, as of last Saturday. For the time being.
Please don't mention it to anyone.'

Philip looked more shocked. 'Oh, Nicola,' he exclaimed. 'My
poor baby.'

'Yes, well, perhaps it was everything I deserved. Perhaps I had
it coming to me. I don't truly know.'

Philip was still looking shocked. 'I met him once, didn't I?'
he said. 'He was waiting for you one evening, when we came
out together. Do I recall a beautiful blonde in dark blue serge?
Mmmm.'

Nicola nodded. 'That sounds right,' she said. 'That type can
be very tricky, darling,' said Philip. 'I should have warned you.'
'It wouldn't have done any good,' said Nicola. 'And then, I haven't
met a type who can't be.'

'No, I haven't either. As it happens.'

'So you see—'

'Men. They're just weird.'

'Perhaps women are too. We wouldn't know.'

They laughed. 'We'd really better go in,' said Nicola. 'I'll come and see you later,' said Philip. 'I'll come and hold your hand.' They got up and paid their respective bills and left the coffee shop. 'Don't tell anyone,' said Nicola. 'I'm trying to present an immaculate exterior.' 'You're a brave girl,' said Philip. 'And I'm another: your secrets will always be safe with me. Chin up, sweetie! Catch you later.' 'Whizzy,' said Nicola.

# 54

'What are you doing in here in the dark?'

'Nothing. Just lying down.'

'Are you tired? Do you want to have supper in bed?'

'No, no. I'll be fine. I'm just getting my strength back.'

'Are you sure you're alright?'

'I'm fine.'

'Shall I leave you alone again?'

'No, stay for a moment.'

Susannah sat down on the end of the bed. Nicola's miracle recovery seemed to have gone into reverse. 'I'm worried about you,' she said.

'I'm fine, truly.'

'Truly?'

'I just need to do something about my clothes. I didn't bring enough.'

'You can borrow mine, if you like.'

'I'll see. You are so kind.'

'Would you like me to collect the rest of your stuff from Notting Hill?'

'No, not yet. Thanks. I'll buy something.'

'We could go shopping on Thursday – didn't you say you were getting Thursday off?'

'Yes. Yes, we might do that.'

Susannah didn't have much spending money so on Thursday they looked for clothes for both of them in the various charity shops of the neighbourhood. Nicola ended up with a large carrier bag full of garments which left to herself she would not by any means have considered. Then they had the satisfaction of washing them all and hanging them out to dry. There were several items which Susannah meant to take with her the next day to Suffolk where she and her husband and child were to spend the Easter week. There was also a small cotton frock printed with pink and blue rabbits which was to be a moving-in present from Nicola, for Chloe. The weather had suddenly become much warmer as it sometimes can at this time of the year and after they had hung up the washing they sat in the garden together in the sunshine.

'Do you feel just a tiny bit happier?' said Susannah. 'Just a tiny bit?' Nicola considered this. 'Just a tiny bit,' she said. 'Wait till you get into those pink jeans,' said Susannah. 'That'll do the trick.' Nicola considered this too. 'You could be right,' she said. 'I'll try it first thing.' 'Or that denim skirt,' said Susannah encouragingly. Nicola laughed. What was she doing with that denim skirt? 'Are you sure about the length?' she asked. 'It looks a wee bit short to me.' 'It should be shorter,' Susannah assured her. 'I should cut it off a bit if I were you.' 'We'll see,' said Nicola.

Guy came out to them. 'Is that red T-shirt for me?' he asked. 'No,' said Susannah, 'it's mine, actually.' 'Oh,' said Guy, 'Can I have one too?'

'That's the only one there is.'

'Oh.'

'Sorry. Anyway, it's too big for you.'

'That's what I want, a big one.'

'Oh dear. Well, perhaps you can have that one – if you clean out the mice's cage *and* tidy your room by the end of the afternoon.'

Guy departed to perform this mission and Susannah sighed. 'I wonder how long it will be,' she said, 'before he will do anything without being bribed? When does one learn that virtue is its own reward?'

'Some people never do.'

'Perhaps he'll learn it in RE.'

'That would be useful knowledge.'

'More useful than learning about salvation, I would have thought.'

'Oh, yes: salvation. *Did* he ever learn the meaning of salvation?'

'I really don't know. We'll ask him when he comes out again.'

Guy did come out again almost immediately, asking where he might find a box in which to house the mice while he cleaned their cage. 'Listen, Guy,' said his mother, 'we were just wondering – do you remember telling us about salvation? Well – have you been told what it means, yet?'

'Sure.'

'And?'

'Well: it means – it *means* – well, it means that instead of dying, you live, for ever – for *ever*. You have eternal life. That's salvation.'

'Sounds okay, so far. How do you get it, though?'

'Well, you have to *believe*. You have to believe in Jesus Christ, as the only-begotten Son of God.'

'Is that all?'

'Well, that's quite a *lot*.'

'I suppose it is, at that.'

'Oh, and, there are probably a few other things you have to do, to make quite sure. I mean, you can't just believe; you have to be really good, you know, and confess your faults; and you have to love your enemies.'

'I knew there'd be a catch.'

Guy's glance began to slide towards the red T-shirt. 'I say,' he said, 'I'd better get on with these mice, or I won't be finished in time.'

'Just one more thing.'

'If it's quick.'

'Do *you* believe?'

'Well,' said Guy, prevaricating, for he had not, so far, settled the question absolutely, 'I might. I mean, probably. I'm not quite sure, yet. I mean – look, can I do the mice now? You said it would be *quick.*'

'Sorry, darling. Okay. Go and do the mice. And your room, remember?'

'Yeah, yeah, I know.' He went. 'Cor!' said Susannah. 'I mean, *cor.* I had no idea they were teaching them theology.'

'It's hardly that.'

'Well, near enough. I mean, at this rate, we'll have a Christian on our hands.'

'It's a danger you run when you send a child to a C of E school.'

'All we wanted was to make sure he got a good education, and that school just happened to be the nearest possibility.'

'Well, God moves in a mysterious way.'

'Anyway, it's early days, I dare say.'

'It'll probably wear off; it's hardly worn *on*, after all.'

'That's true. No need to get the wind up.'

'It wears off most people, I imagine.' Jonathan, for example.

'That's true too, probably.'

'Still: salvation. Not such a bad deal, is it?'

'I don't know – perhaps it isn't. It's just—'

'I know what you mean.'

'I mean, the whole thing's simply preposterous.'

'Yes, it is, absolutely.'

But that, she suddenly suspected, might be its chiefest recommendation. 'You wouldn't think anyone could *ever* believe that stuff, would you?' she said, marvelling. 'Let alone in these days.'

'Even quite intelligent people. Otherwise intelligent, anyway.'
'It's an utter mystery.'
'Yes, it is. An *utter* mystery.'

# 55

He'd been almost glad to come down to Gloucestershire this time: the flat was getting on his nerves. Of course, he could have gone somewhere else. He could have gone to any number of places, he had Europe at his feet. A whole four days: he could even have gone to New York, why not? Now that was a good question. Jonathan had come up against several good questions lately: a good question being one which has no apparent answer. So he had come down to Gloucestershire on this Easter Saturday, and now his mother was making some tea.

'Your father is conferring with Charles Anstruther,' she said; 'he'll be back in a while and we can have some lunch.' She picked up the tea-tray. 'I thought we might have this in the garden,' she said. 'The tulips are all up, it's looking so lovely. You got here just in time for them.' 'Let me take that,' said Jonathan. He took the tea-tray and they went outside.

'I'm surprised you're not spending Easter together,' said Sophie carefully, pouring tea. 'You and Nicola. She is quite well, is she?'

'We're not together any longer,' said Jonathan shortly. 'Nicola and I have parted company.'

Sophie put down the teapot. 'Oh dear!' she cried. 'How dreadful!' These exclamations had escaped her as it were involuntarily; she was even it appeared surprised at having heard herself utter them. 'Oh, do forgive me,' she said hastily. 'Of course you must know what you are doing better than I. I had no business – please, take no notice. Oh dear.' 'It doesn't matter,' said Jonathan. Sophie was pink with confusion. A degree of alarm had seized her: she could not recover from the sensation that Jonathan's words had provoked: she could only see the news as dreadful. She finished pouring the tea. 'I don't understand,' she said weakly. 'You seemed such a happy couple. I thought – well, there you are. My thoughts are beside the point, I know.' Jonathan drank some tea and said nothing. 'Biscuit?' said Sophie, handing the plate. Jonathan simply shook his head, the teacup at his lips. 'Nice tea,' he said. 'Is it Darjeeling?'

'Yes,' said Sophie sadly. 'You know your father. He simply refuses to drink any other kind.' She drank some herself. She still felt quite acutely distressed. Nicola had not been ideal, perhaps no one ever could have been, but she had been nice: that was as much as one could really dare to ask. Sophie could not see how an intimate relationship between two nice people could possibly come adrift. This should by rights have concluded with an engagement to be married, not a separation. There was something dark, mysterious, wrong here: it filled her with fresh alarm and fear. What might one say? All her questions seemed impertinent. There were huge tracts of forbidden ground between mothers and sons. She stole a look at hers: his face was blank; it told her nothing. There was at any rate the matter of the flat; curiosity on that point at least was permissible. 'You haven't left the flat, then – have you? Or has Nicola—' 'No,' Jonathan said. 'I'm taking over Nicola's share of the mortgage. She's moved out. We could have done it the other way around, but she couldn't afford it.'

The coldness of this startled even Jonathan himself, now that the words were out, here, now. This was the first conversation he had had on the subject since the situation had arisen. That there would be other people who must be told, that it would be he who must tell them, was an aspect of it which had not initially occurred to him. He had not foreseen how unpleasant it could be: how unpleasant to hear himself saying these words. One almost had an image of Nicola wrapped in a shawl, driven out into the snow. It was quite ridiculous, of course; he banished it from his mind, and with it all lesser suggestions of pathos or misfortune. 'She'll buy something else,' he said, re-establishing her image as a woman of substance and resource; a free agent, just like himself. 'It shouldn't be difficult to find something suitable.'

But Sophie, unable to ask any of the questions which clamoured in her mind, alive therefore to all chance clues and inferences, heard in these words some small part of the answer she sought. 'I dare say this is not quite as she might have planned, though,' she said very tentatively. 'I mean, it does seem rather sad for her to have to leave that lovely flat that you'd both worked on so much.' This was Jonathan's chance to assure her that the parting was at Nicola's instigation; he did not do so. 'That's life,' he said abruptly. 'It often doesn't work out according to plan. We all have to take our chances.'

'I'm sorry,' she said. 'Don't be,' said Jonathan. 'There is absolutely nothing to be sorry for. If you think there is then you've misunderstood the situation completely. We were both free of any responsibility except to ourselves. We weren't married, we had no children. We were free to do as we liked. So we did.' 'Yes, of course,' said Sophie. But she didn't agree, not for a minute. That she should attempt to argue the point with Jonathan, however, was entirely out of the question. 'Would you like some more tea?' she said. And so the subject, dark and fearful as it remained, was closed.

# 56

'New car, Mother.'

'Yes, we thought we'd treat ourselves. Your father says it's a retirement present.'

'But that's not till next year.'

'You know how impatient he can be. Vroom. Listen to that. Nought to sixty in three seconds, or something of the kind. He calls me Mrs Toad. We'll go for a proper spin later, you can have a go.'

'Lovely.'

'Why the dieting, Nicola?'

'What dieting?'

'You seem to have lost about a stone since we last saw you.'

'You know how short the skirts are this year.'

'It doesn't suit you. You look terrible.'

'Now I feel terrible too. Perhaps you'd better take me back to the station.'

'Not before I've fed you up. See, here we are. No point in going back before you've had some cake. I made one just for you. Can you manage that? Let's go in then.'

They went inside, and into the kitchen. Elinor put the kettle on and they sat down. 'What is it, Nicola?' she said. She had suddenly thought: oh dear, she couldn't be pregnant, could she? But that might even turn out to be a good thing. 'It's nothing much,' said Nicola. 'It's just, that Jonathan and I have parted.' 'Oh, never!' cried Elinor. 'Yes,' said Nicola. 'He's decided that he doesn't love me. After all. He's going to buy me out. I've left the flat already, actually. I'm staying with Susannah. It's alright, really. I've found a sort of pied-à-terre near to her and Geoffrey, with some friends of theirs. I'm moving in at the end of next week. They've got a baby girl called Chloe. I'll buy another flat eventually. I've just been feeling a bit of shock, that's all. It all happened so suddenly. I'm fine, really. The kettle's boiling, did you know?'

Elinor got up to make the tea and Nicola sat twisting her hanky around her fingers. It was a long time since she had last cried; she had not thought that she would do so again, but tears were coming into her eyes now. In fact they were even starting to fall. Elinor put the teapot on the table and got the other accoutrements together. She sat down again. 'My poor darling. I am so sorry.' Nicola began to cry in earnest, and her mother after a moment or two began to cry too. Her father came in: he had been out with the dog. 'What on earth is going on here?' he said. Elinor cast a despairing look at her daughter, as if to say, will you tell him or shall I? Nicola blew her nose. 'Hello, Pa,' she said. 'It's Jonathan. He's – we've separated. As it were. So we were just having a cry. It's nothing, really.'

'Oh, if you say so,' said Michael. '*I* should have said it was *something*. I've got a good mind to take a shotgun to him. That is – this *was* his idea, I take it? Judging by the fact that you're in tears.' 'Yes,' said Nicola. 'Although for all we know it's still my fault.'

'Of that I can't see the slightest chance,' said Michael. 'It's his fault, and he's a rotter. I said he should have married you and had done. Now look. These new-fangled schemes are all very well, but they don't work.' He sat down, genuinely and deeply perturbed, and Elinor poured out the tea. 'I don't understand how it could have happened,' she said. 'I thought you were so happy together.' 'So did I,' said Nicola sadly. 'It seems that I was wrong. At least, latterly.' She gave them an edited account of the events of the past fortnight.

'That Jonathan has a problem,' said Elinor firmly. 'The chap's one slice short of a sandwich,' said Michael. 'Or even very possibly two slices.' 'We should have seen it,' said Elinor. 'He was well camouflaged,' said Michael. 'One has a ridiculous prejudice in favour of people wearing traditional costume. Better try one of these chaps with spiky hair and black boots next time round, he might take proper care of you.' Nicola began to laugh and then to cry again. 'There, there,' said Elinor. 'Don't listen to your father. Let's have some cake. Can you get it, Michael? It's in the pantry.' They had an old-fashioned house with a pantry, a scullery, and an ingle nook fireplace: someone had once told them it might be a Voysey, but they hadn't attempted to verify the attribution.

The dog had been licking the tears from his beloved Nicola's hands but was now diverted by the appearance of the cake. They gave him a small piece and then ordered him to sit down, which he did, casting them a look of terrible pathos. 'Good Asterix,' they said. He was a large black poodle. Nicola ate some cake too. She was glad enough, now that the process had begun, to sink back into the position of daughter of the house, cherished youngest child. She had never been rebellious or difficult; it had never been necessary or even desirable. Elinor outlined her tentative plans for the weekend and Nicola acceded to them. They would visit her sister Rosemary twenty miles away; while there they might telephone her brother Simon who was working in New Zealand – they did hope he wouldn't decide in the end to settle there – it did seem a good chance, while they were all together and could all put in a word, and wish him a happy Easter, so far away.

They might go for that spin, in a wee while, if Nicola felt up to it. 'Of course I do, Ma,' she said. 'I'm not *sick*.' 'No, of course not,' said Elinor. 'But I dare say you're suffering from shock. It's only a fortnight, since – didn't you say? Shock can leave a person feeling awfully weak. I know.' 'I suppose so,' said Nicola. 'We'll go to the sea,' said Elinor. 'That will make you feel better. Nothing like the sea for that.' So they did, and, as a matter of fact, it did, for a while, up to a point.

# 57

'How many Easter eggs did you get?'

'Only the one. From my parents.'

Nicola had never stopped hoping that Jonathan might awaken from the nightmare into which he had dragged her. She had hoped – only now was this illusion in tatters – that he might appear at Susannah's front door, Easter egg in hand: an immensely rare creation from which when it was cracked open a dove would fly, heralding resurrection.

'*I* got three.'

'Lucky old you.'

'One of them was French.'

'Luckier still.'

'I saved some for you.'

'Have you got it with you?'

'No, it's at home. We thought we might ask you round on Friday night, if you're free.'

'I am, as a matter of act. Who's *we*?'

One never knew, with Philip. He was always falling for someone new.

'Me and Jean-Claude. Hence the French Easter egg. Fresh from Paris.'

'Yummy.'

'Yes, wait till you see him. Supposing he's still around, by Friday. We might go clubbing. *Clerbing*. Do you fancy that?'

'I don't know.'

'Then you'd better give it a try. I'll come and fetch you here on Friday evening, okay? And we'll whizz away together.'

So she had something to think about after she got back to the empty house in Clapham after work on Tuesday. Clothes, for clubbing. What did one wear to such places? It was hopeless. She ate a sketchy meal and watched television, and waited for the telephone to ring, knowing that it would not: it was hopeless, hopeless. But how did one relinquish such hopes—hopeless as they might be—how could one, while one breathed?

On Wednesday evening she did all Susannah's ironing, as well as her own. She ironed Chloe's rabbit-printed frock and put it aside; the telephone rang.

It was Susannah.

'Are you alright?'

'I'm fine.'

'What are you doing?'

'I've been ironing. What about you?'

'We're having fun. I wish you were here. What else are you doing?'

'I'm going clubbing on Friday night.'

'Never.'

'Truly. Philip at work is taking me, with his new boyfriend Jean-Claude.'

'Now you're talking. Don't let them give you any of those weird pills, I'm sure they're dangerous.'

'Of course not.'


'Have some of this,' said Philip. 'It's the Friday night special.' The Friday night special was an extremely long joint, rather badly rolled; but it did the trick. 'I haven't had any of this for simply ages,' said Nicola. 'Hmmm,' said Philip. 'I guess not.'

He put on some strange music and started tidying up the sitting room, in the course of which activity he found a hat which – seeing no more logical place for it – he put on Nicola's head. 'You can have that,' he said. 'It never did a thing for me.' It was a black velvet pillbox with silver embroidery around the sides and a silver knob on the crown. In due course Jean-Claude, a young man beautiful and elegant in the standard-issue French style, emerged from the kitchen and invited them to come and have some soup. Then they had biscuits and several different kinds of cheese, and another spliff. Philip played some more strange music and told Nicola to stand up and let him have a good look at her. 'I don't want any trouble at the door,' he said.

She stood still as ordered. She was wearing the denim skirt and a white shirt. 'Hmmm' said Philip. He and Jean-Claude discussed clubs, which they should and should not visit that evening, and this question having been at last decided Philip took a harder look. 'You're not ideologically committed to that skirt length, are you?' he asked. Nicola told him that she was not. 'Then we'll change it if you don't mind,' he said. 'Now where did I put my scissors?'

She stood still while he cut three inches off the bottom of the skirt. 'Fishnet stockings,' he said. He disappeared and came back with some fishnet tights and a silver leather waistcoat. 'I think you'll just about do,' he said. Put these on and let's have a look. Keep the hat on.' Nicola did as she was told. 'Red,' he said. 'She needs some red.' He went away again and after a while came back with some lipstick and nail varnish. 'Red Devil,' he said. 'Guaranteed to inflame. You do the nails, Jean-Claude, your young hands are so much steadier than mine. Take off the fishnets, darling, we've got to do the toenails as well.' 'But no one will see them,' she protested. 'Is that any reason?' asked Philip. 'God can see them. Take 'em off like a good girl and sit down.'

She did as she'd been told, and so did Jean-Claude. '*Que tu as les pieds jolis,*' he enthused. 'That's enough of that,' said Philip. 'Just concentrate on your work.' He put on some more music and went to make some coffee. 'A little caffeine at this stage,' he said. 'We've got to move it along.'

He came back and painted her mouth, took the hat off and pinned her hair back behind her ears and then replaced the hat. Her nails were all painted by now and she was waiting for them to dry. Philip brought in the coffee, with the remains of the French Easter egg and some nondescript-looking pills. 'Take one of these,' he said. 'It'll keep you on your feet.' She could hardly refuse. She put the fishnet tights on again and drank some coffee. 'Be careful of the *maquillage*,' said Philip; she was. 'Well,' he said, 'let's have one last good look at you. Stand over there.' She did so: it was wonderful, not having to think, not having to make decisions, simply taking orders; wonderful. 'Hmmm,' said Philip. 'Ear-rings.' 'I can't,' she said. 'My ears aren't pierced.' '*What?*' exclaimed Philip. '*What* did you say? I never heard of such a thing. I could do it for you now.' 'No,' said Nicola; 'please don't.' 'Well don't blame me,' said Philip, 'if they won't let you in.'

But they did; in the first place, and the second, and the third. 'Okay,' said Philip. 'Let's go out there and show these babies how to boogie.' And that, as far as Nicola was concerned, was what they did. You never, but never, saw anything like it in your life. If she'd known for a moment that London was actually pot-holed by these vast fantastical spaces filled with people dancing – as if in devotion to some god – which they were, in a way: if she'd known this, then she wouldn't be where she was today; or was it tonight; or was it in fact the next day up?

And if she'd known, and not, therefore, been here, today, tonight, tomorrow, or whatever it was, well then – what? And Jean-Claude: he was just – *tu vois* – entirely perfect: when she lost her hat, once, *he found it again*. In amongst all these people – hundreds of them, all dancing – he found her hat. Just cop that.

# 58

They emerged into the pastel pre-dawn light, the streets of the West End around them almost empty, freshly-washed, clean and innocent. The air was full of birdsong. 'Isn't it beautiful?' said Nicola in wonder. 'It's so *beautiful*.' The street lamps were still alight, golden spangles in the pellucid haze. 'If we take a stroll down through the park,' said Philip, 'we should hit Westminster Bridge just about sunrise time: how about that? We'll do like Wordsworth.'

They leaned on the balustrade, looking downriver, and waited for the miracle. Big Ben struck the half-hour, and a few minutes later it arrived. They all saw that they were fortunate beyond all reckoning and were silent. Quite soon the sun was well up, and the din of traffic increased; a launch passed noisily under the bridge: the morning began to slide into banality. Nicola turning her head saw a taxi approaching from the Lambeth end of the bridge. 'I think I might go for that,' she told them. 'Thank you. For everything. With all my heart.' Kisses were exchanged; Philip hailed the cab and they all crossed the road. 'Will you be alright?' he said. She got in and smiled at them through the window. 'Absolutely,' she said; she waved a last farewell as the taxi did a U-turn. It was almost precisely a fortnight since she'd last sat in the back of a taxi crossing the river southwards: and this time she was not trying not to cry: this time, she was actually smiling. She was astonished by this. She was smiling: underneath, at the bottom of her heart, a perpetual flame of anguish still burned;

but at a more immediate level of sensation she was feeling what she would have thought impossible: happiness.

There was so much music still going on inside her head that she thought she would just sit down here in the sitting-room for a while and listen to some more. Of course Geoffrey and Susannah hadn't any of the kind she'd been dancing to but she looked through their collection and chose something which she thought might be complementary at any rate, and she put it on and went into the kitchen and made some tea. Then she sat on the sofa, and thought about the night which had just gone by, and the miraculous morning, and listened to the music, and marvelled at this sensation of happiness which still enveloped her: until suddenly, just like that, feeling ever so tired, suddenly, she lay down, just for a minute; and fell fast asleep.

Some time later she was awakened, by a ringing – was it the telephone? She started up: there was silence, and then the bell sounded once more: the front door. Oh dear. It could be the milkman: the account was settled on Saturdays – she'd been warned; she'd promised to see to it. Her hat had fallen on the floor; she picked it up and put it on again; this seemed at the moment the reasonable thing to do. Pulling her extremely short skirt straight, she went to the door, and opened it.

'Hello, Nicola.'

'Oh!'

'I thought I ought to bring you these.'

Jonathan: Jonathan, of whom she had despaired. Jonathan, with her mail.

'That was very good of you. Will you come in?' Jonathan, here, now.

'Well, just for a moment.'

Nicola led the way into the sitting-room. They both stood there awkwardly and she gestured at the sofa. 'Won't you sit down?' He sat down very gingerly and looked around, not with

Sam's frankly inquisitive stare but with a sort of trepidation, as if he expected the faces of gnomes and elves suddenly to appear, grinning spitefully. 'Are you alone?' he asked. 'Yes. They're all away on holiday still. They're coming back this afternoon some time.' She didn't know what to say, what to do. 'I was going to make some tea,' she improvised. 'Will you have some?' 'No,' he said; 'thank you all the same. But do go ahead.' 'It doesn't matter,' she said. 'It can wait.' Although she had slept for only a few hours, she felt a strange clarity.

She saw what was bothering him just before he spoke. 'Have you been at a party?' he said. 'No. Dancing. I didn't get back until a short time ago – I haven't actually been to bed yet. We were clubbing.' 'Oh.' 'I went with Philip, from work. And a friend of his.' 'Oh, yes.' He knew what sort of friend *that* was. She saw that he didn't want to know what she had been doing; the question had been a formality. He didn't want to hear the answer.

He wondered now what he was doing here: and so did she. 'You really needn't have brought the mail,' she said, rather stiffly. 'You could have re-addressed it.' 'I thought you might need it straight away,' he said. 'I think they send re-addressed letters second class.' 'Well, thank you,' she said, listlessly looking through the bunch. 'I'll do something about a proper redirection next week.' There was a letter from Scunthorpe.

'I could have brought your other things too,' he went on. 'But I wasn't sure whether you wanted them yet.' 'No,' she said, 'I'll collect them myself in a week or two. I've found a couple of rooms to rent, near here. Friends of Susannah and Geoffrey.' 'Oh, good,' he said. He didn't want to know: she could see that he had hardly taken in what she had said. She was hard against the great blank wall of his indifference. 'Well–' she said. 'If that's all–?' 'Yes,' he said. 'I only came to bring the mail.' He hesitated for a moment and then got up. Then he seemed to think of something more to say after all. 'You're not still feeling resentful about what's happened, I hope,' he said. 'I never intended any enmity towards you and I would have hoped that you'd feel none towards me. I don't know whether we can be friends but I never wished or expected that we'd become enemies.'

She was, properly, astounded: but her mind still felt as clear as ice. 'You must be living in a dream world,' she said. 'Words like friends, enemies, enmity, resentment, don't begin to apply in the real world where I've been, the last few weeks. But I don't suppose there's any use in our trying to talk about this, in the circumstances.'

Some trace of a genuine emotion seemed to have gripped him. 'I can't seem to make you realise that I've done what was right not only for me but for you too,' he said. He wasn't indifferent any longer. 'It seems never to have occurred to you, that entering into a permanent relationship, e.g. marriage, e.g. parenthood, is probably more dangerous than walking across a minefield. And the possible suffering is more prolonged, and affects everyone near you. When it isn't absolutely right it's absolutely wrong. And *when* it's *absolutely wrong* you've got your back against the wall for the rest of your life. Did you really want to risk that?'

'Yes,' she said. 'I loved you. That's what it means, to love someone: to be willing to take that risk.'

'Then love is only a kind of insanity,' he said. 'So be it,' she replied. 'You see, it's not a case now of resentment, or enmity, or etcetera, it's a case of mutual incomprehension. There's too large an accumulation of doubt and fear which you might have talked about at the time when it first came into your mind but which you simply harboured in secret. I suppose it's been sitting there for months earning compound interest and now it's too large to see beyond. It's all there is.' She paused. 'It's over,' she said.

She hadn't quite known all these things before saying them, but as she had done so she saw that they were true, as far as they went. Jonathan's silence had been a kind of infidelity and her misapprehension of his state of mind had been a kind of hubris and now they were both alone. He had continued to stand, as had she; he was leaning now against Susannah's mantelpiece, looking down at the objects on it as if puzzled by them – as he might in fact have been: some large ivory chess pieces, a bronze candlestick, a small vase of dying flowers and a painting, propped against the mirror, of Guy's. He was silent for a moment; he seemed to be thinking about what she'd said. But when he spoke, it was from behind the wall of indifference once more.

'As you say,' he said. 'It's over; yes.' He straightened up. 'It's time I was going,' he said. 'I'll be in touch soon about the sale – sorry I haven't been quicker off the mark there but I've been terribly tied up at work, there's hardly been a moment. I'll get it sorted out this week, that's a promise.' 'You can call me at work,' she said. 'Yes, right, I will,' he replied. He followed her from the room and into the hallway; she opened the front door and he crossed the threshold, and then half turned back. 'Good-bye then,' he said. 'Good-bye.' She shut the door and went back into the sitting-room and sat hunched over on the sofa, nursing the new and horrific pain which now had possession of her. All the happiness she had felt had fled. *It's over.* She had said it, she herself. It was true.

# 59

'So then I went upstairs and had a bath and got dressed and then I slept for a while. And then I went shopping and came back and made this cake and then you came home. Thank God.'

'Terrific cake.'

'Least I could do.'

'Show me this hat.'

Nicola fetched the hat. 'Put it on.' She did as bidden. 'Mmmm,' said Susannah. 'Delightful. I'm just trying to visualise the whole effect. Fishnet tights and all. Well, all I can say is, it must have given him a right old turn. No wonder he was acting so cold and indifferent. He was actually *steaming*.'

Nicola seemed to consider this proposition for a moment and then she gave a small dismissive shrug. 'It's over, Susannah,' she said. 'It really is. I know it now. It's over.' Susannah looked suitably grave. 'Do you mean,' she said carefully, 'that you no longer love him?' 'No,' said Nicola. 'I mean that my loving him – if I do – has no significance any longer. If ever it had. It's so insignificant that even I can see it to be so. Everything I feel, everything I am, is swallowed up by Jonathan's indifference. Even if his indifference is assumed. *Especially* if it is assumed.'

'Still,' said Susannah, 'he did come here. Doesn't that indicate something besides indifference? He needn't really have come here, in person, unless—'

'I've thought about that too. Do you know why he came here? Because he was actually hoping to assure himself that everything was right between us: I mean, nice, calm, dignified. Even friendly. No hard feelings. In other words, he had a very slightly bad conscience. He wanted to be *told* that he'd done the right thing, as well as merely believing it himself. He wanted to feel good. That's why he came here.'

'Poor old Jonathan,' said Susannah. 'His back is against the wall whatever he does.'

'Still, he has his work, to take his mind off. One needn't feel too sorry for him. He only notices the wall at weekends, and possibly now and then in the evenings. Somehow my work never seems to do as much for me, quite.'

'We women still have a lot of catching up to do.'

'We have to learn to be more single-minded.'

'Tougher. More ambitious. *Ruthless.*'

'I've been shortlisted for that Scunthorpe thing, by the way. I have an interview on Friday week.'

'You won't *get* it, will you?'

'Of course not.'

'Do you promise?'

'Cross my heart.'

'I wonder how they're getting on round at Cardamon Road. Or whether they are. We might pop round there tomorrow and check it out – what do you say?'

'I might give them a hand.'

'That seems a bit much.'

'We'll see.'

And they did. The consequence was that Nicola did indeed give them a hand; on two of the following evenings she went round after work and did a large amount of cleaning, and on two of the evenings following these she gave a hand with the painting, too, and so did Guy, after a fashion. What they were doing was putting white emulsion straight on to the original *in situ* 1950s *moderne* wallpaper, the Festival of Britain-style pattern of which began soon to peep through, creating a most interesting new wall-treatment effect at a time when every other previously dreamed up by decorators (ragging, marbling, you-name-it) had been consigned to the *vieux jeu* bin. But they agreed that they would divulge the secret of it to no one, and it remained unique, not only in fashionable Clapham but in the entire 0171 telephone exchange area.

# 60

If Sam had contemplated pulling in his horns, it had still to be admitted that they'd been stuck as far out as horns can go.

The house had a basement, which he had renovated to form a kitchen and dark-room for his and Helen's photography: they being dedicated amateurs. 'Although, of course,' said Sam, 'there's not the slightest hope of our finding time for it until Chloe shapes up, which event – extrapolating from present trends – I do not anticipate before the end of the century.' Where Susannah and Geoffrey had a kitchen, they had a conservatory, but the rest of the ground floor was occupied by the same kind of knocked-through sitting-room, Hodgkin-less as it might be.

Now it was Friday evening and everyone was in there drinking supermarket Côtes du Rhône and discussing Nicola's furniture. 'She can have Chloe's bed,' said Sam. 'Chloe's still using a cot. She won't be needing that bed for the foreseeable. I just need a hand moving it up the stairs, when you're ready, Geoffrey.' 'Right away,' said Geoffrey. 'Well, I didn't mean this very minute,' said Sam crossly. 'I mean, let's have just one more glass first.' He poured out some more wine, and opened another bottle as well, and sat down again.

The women were all sitting together on the sofa, Chloe – dressed in the rabbit-printed frock – crawling over their collective knees and being saved from falling by whichever hand was nearest at the relevant time, and Guy was sitting pathetically in a corner looking at an atlas and drinking orange squash. Susannah spoke up. 'What about the floor?' she said. 'Do you need a rug?' 'A rug,' said Sam, as if he'd never heard of such a thing. 'It's alright,' said Nicola hastily. 'I don't need one.' 'Of course you do,' said Helen. 'You must have a rug.' 'She can have Chloe's,' said Sam. 'Chloe can do without. She doesn't know the difference, do you, Chloe?' 'Yeah,' said Chloe. She was on the very verge of talking: she was already using sentences, but had picked up only a few essential words; the rest she improvised. If asked a question she usually said yeah. After some discussion it was agreed that in lieu of the first week's rent Nicola herself would see to a floor covering and something for the windows, and Susannah promised to take her around the shops the next day in order to accomplish this feat.

'She'll need a wardrobe, of course,' said Helen. Everyone's faces fell. Here at last was an insoluble problem: what on earth should they do? 'I know where there's a wardrobe,' said Guy. He did, too. It was usually on the pavement outside a very dismal junk shop which he passed on the way to and from school every day. 'It probably isn't there now,' said Susannah. 'It's been there for *weeks*,' said Guy. 'It's *always* there.' 'It must be very ugly,' said Susannah. 'Oh, yes, it is,' Guy agreed. 'But it is a wardrobe.' So on the way to Guy's riding lesson the next morning they checked it out. It was still there, and it was very ugly, but they got it very cheap, and the vendor agreed to deliver it that evening, which he did.

'She'll want a chair, of course,' said Geoffrey. 'And a table.' 'She's got those in the kitchen,' said Sam. 'Two chairs, in point of fact. Two.' 'I don't need any more,' said Nicola. 'Truly. The less furniture the better.' What else could she say, could she truly, miserably feel, who had walked away for ever from a discreetly magnificent bed, Empire style, bought in glad hope at a Liberty's sale: to say nothing of all the rest? Then Sam and Geoffrey went upstairs to move the bed; the women came up to see how it looked; Nicola lay on it to convince them that she found it comfortable; Guy lay on it too in order to see for himself; and then they discussed bedding. 'I've got my own sheets,' said Nicola. So the rest they managed to find, and Helen promised to make available some of the kitchen crockery and utensils. They were all sorted out at last, and Nicola was to move in on Sunday.

# 61

A few more letters had come for Nicola: Jonathan hesitated. Hadn't she mentioned something about moving? But she hadn't given him an address. And he hadn't asked for it. He quite literally didn't know where she was, unless she was still with Susannah. Well, he'd just have to forward the mail to Susannah's house. He sat down with the letters and began to re-address them c/o Mrs Geoffrey Dawlish.

By the end of the week, the supply seemed to have dried up: she'd evidently notified the Post Office; he wouldn't need to take care of her mail any longer. And next week he'd finish re-arranging the mortgage and he would pay her off – so to speak – and that would be the lot.

Except for those boxes in the wardrobe. Presumably she would soon collect them as promised. And then she'd really be gone, thoroughly and finally *gone*. Jonathan had a rare instant of unflinching honesty. How did it feel? To have her gone, thoroughly, finally? Oh, it felt wretched, wretched. And that could only be a trick of the light, a devilish deception, a cross one had to bear for having done what was right. It had been simple-minded of him to expect that he should feel, as well as be, right. That surely would come. Soon he would no longer feel that blank, odd, wrong sensation when he came into the sitting-room and saw the empty mantelpiece – soon he would think of something to replace the vanished – banished? – dogs: he couldn't for the moment imagine what, precisely. Soon he would wake up feeling himself, his soul not only his, not only private and inviolate, but intact and securely in its proper place. Everything would be, and would be felt to be, clear and tidy and absolutely right.

In any case, the wretchedness he might feel now – which was only a trick of the light – was preferable by far and even welcome when compared to the certain and enduring hell of marriage as it might very well turn out to be. As it was altogether likely to be. Jonathan knew now what he had for a very long time suspected, and had turned away from: that human life, at least the way one lived it here and now, was a fraud, driven by irrational and potentially destructive forces, and the only reasonable and safe course was to minimise the chances of harming and being harmed. He was beginning to arrive at the quietist position, joylessly, regretfully, wretchedly. He even glimpsed the possibility that there was some factor he had overlooked, but he did not stop to ask what it might be.

He suddenly, unaccountably, remembered the beautiful ruby ring. Where did that fit into the scheme of things? One had to admire the resourcefulness of those dread irrational forces: there were no lengths to which they might not go in order to lure you into hell. On their behalf rubies were mined, traded, cut and polished, set, traded again; insured, inherited; he could almost smile at the fate that had brought this one, so anomalously, into his hand. Issa would end up getting it after all. He could just see – for a very brief, agonised instant – that in point of fact (now he came, for the first time, to think of it) Nicola would have loved it. But this detail, of course, was only there to compound the irony.

What was it she'd said about compound interest? What should he have said and done that he had failed to say and do? And he remembered her red – ruby-red – fingernails. She – this was another irony – had moved on into a new life, and he was still in the old one! Wretched, and thinking of her – although he did not love her, and could not marry her: and more sure than ever that sexual desire (for he had to admit to that, too) was the most irrational and destructive force of all, the drug that induced one into the very worst mistakes one could ever make, mistakes whose consequences went on for all of time. It was unspeakable. Better this misery than that. Jonathan, at last, embraced the rational misery he had chosen. So be it, he said to himself. And then he got on with some work.

# 62

'Perhaps I should do it with gloss.'

'No, emulsion's okay. Do it with emulsion. Emulsion's better.'

'And we've got emulsion. Emulsion's easier.'

Nicola had just moved in, and she and Susannah and Helen were discussing the wardrobe, which all agreed should be painted white. Otherwise the room looked quite nice, with maize matting on the floor and split-cane blinds at the windows. Nicola had bought a simple reading lamp in the same shop, with a paper shade.

'You need a plant,' said Susannah. 'I'll get you one for a housewarming present. And you haven't got a radio either. You can borrow mine from the workroom if you like. Let's go home now and have some dinner and I'll see if there are any more bits and pieces you could use.' 'You're so kind,' said Nicola faintly. 'I'm sure I've got all the necessities.' She wanted to live like an anchorite now, stripped of everything inessential.

She returned later that night with a radio, some tea-towels, a travelling alarm clock, an extra pillow, a tin-opener, a corkscrew and a bottle of wine. 'Now promise me,' said Susannah in the car, 'that if it turns out to be horrible in there, you'll come straight back to us.' 'I'll be fine,' said Nicola. 'But promise,' Susannah insisted. 'After all, you never know. Sam's a sardonic old sod and Helen can be awfully shrewish.' 'But Chloe's a pet,' said Nicola. 'It'll be fine. I must go in and get straightened out. Work again tomorrow.' 'Okay,' said Susannah sadly. 'Take care, sweetheart.'

Because she was truly concerned about Nicola. She felt as strongly as ever she had, that what had happened to Nicola ought not to have happened, that it was as completely unjust as such a thing could be: that what had happened was truly wrong. She said all this to Geoffrey when she got home.

'Well, if it's as wrong as all that,' he said, 'then it's right.'

'How can that be?'

'Well, if Jonathan could perpetrate so abominable an injustice, she's well out of it. It's a jolly good thing he did. Otherwise she might have been shacked up with the monster for ever.'

'But if he hadn't done it he wouldn't *be* a monster.'

'Oh, you mean he became a monster after he did it. Or at least, while he did it. That he wasn't one before.'

'Well—'

'I mean, logically, he had to be a monster before he did it, or he couldn't have done it. There has to be the will before the action can be performed.'

'Well, he could have just had the monstrous will but then thought better of the action and not performed it.'

'So you'd rather he were a devious hypocritical secretive monster.'

'No, I'd rather he were a reformed monster who has seen the error of his wishes and not turned them into actions.'

'It seems a lot to ask of a monster.'

'What's the point of being a monster if one doesn't reform oneself?'

'What's the point of being a monster if one does?'

'He shouldn't have pretended not to be a monster to start with. That would have been best.'

'Yes, well.'

'Why are men so awful?'

'Because they're bipeds.'

'What do you mean?'

'Just think about it. What's the really startling difference between men and dogs, or cats, or any other male mammal?'

'*Oh.*'

'You see? Vulnerable.'

'It's tragic, really.'

'That's life, human-style.'

'Funny, isn't it.'

'Hilarious.'

# 63

'Nicola! Are you up there?'

Nicola, paintbrush in hand, went out on to the landing. It was Sam, coming up the stairs with a sizeable pot-plant shrouded in florist's wrapping paper. 'Ah,' he said. 'Just brought this up for you. Guy delivered it this afternoon while you were still out at work. Dashed useful child, that. Unlike some. Where shall I put it?' He was invited to come in and Nicola took the plant and unwrapped it. It was a white pelargonium, perfectly beautiful, with a card from Susannah. 'What a dear friend she is,' murmured Nicola. 'Yes,' said Sam. 'I dare say she is. You women go in for that sort of thing, don't you?' Nicola wasn't sure what sort of thing was meant here, but said that she supposed they did, and put the plant on the mantelpiece above the unlit gas fire.

Sam looked around the room with his usual beady-eyed glare. 'Looks alright, doesn't it?' he said proudly – his being the least of the efforts which had been expended upon it. Nicola smiled to herself and agreed with him, and recommenced her painting of the wardrobe. 'Yes,' said Sam approvingly, 'that's the ticket. If it doesn't move, paint it white. My father was in the regular army, did you know that? No, don't get the idea that he was officer class. Up through the ranks. Staff sergeant. Bloody hell. Still, he survived and so did I.' He looked around the room again. 'Not exactly overburdened with possessions, are you?' he said. Nicola agreed that she was not, and was tempted to leave it at that, but then relented. 'I've abandoned them,' she explained.

'But in fact there are a few more to come. I have to fetch them from Notting Hill some time soon.' 'Oh, yes,' said Sam. 'Notting Hill.' What more need one say? Nicola felt a sudden wrenching in her stomach. Notting Hill. The pain could even now (*it's over*) intensify in this way, as if renewing itself, as if resurrecting itself, and tighten its grip with a force more terrible still than before.

'Oh, by the way,' said Sam – aware, perhaps merely at some subliminal level, of the change in the atmosphere – 'I don't know if you've anything particular lined up in the way of food, but if you haven't then Helen suggested you might eat with us this evening. We dine at around eight o'clock.' Nicola thanked him and said that she would bring a bottle of wine which she happened to have handy, and Sam, looking around the room one last time as if to catch sight after all of some enviable item of luxury, some *objet de* – doubtful – *virtu*, withdrew.

Nicola went on with the painting. There was one thing about the smell of fresh paint: even if it reminded one of happier – midsummer-sky-blue – times, it was still an encouraging, optimistic, even joyful sort of smell; she hardly knew how she could have borne her situation, here, now, without it.

# 64

The note which she received at work on Tuesday morning was hand-written on the firm's stationery.

Dear Nicola,

The paperwork *in re* the mortgage transfer is now in order, so if you could call in here later in the week and sign on the relevant dotted lines the sale can be finalised. I suggest Thursday at around 1 p.m. – let me know if you would prefer a different day or time or both.

Yours,
Jonathan

Dear Jonathan,

The time you suggest is as good as any – I will see you then.

Nicola

And now she was on the top of a bus – because it was more amusing than the tube, and there was no other amusement here to be had – crawling through the lunch-hour traffic towards the City, and Jonathan, and the finalising of the sale, and it's just a task to be performed, she told herself, a mere detail: not the worst, not even the last to be tidied away: it will take only a few minutes.

She was kept waiting for two of these minutes at the reception desk, and then Jonathan appeared. He nodded and did not quite smile, and she followed him down a corridor and into his office. He had quite a large one these days, it appeared. The furniture seemed rather good: a knee-hole desk with a leather top, even a wing chair in a corner. For a dowager, say. Did Jonathan deal with dowagers? It was not altogether out of the question. There was probably a bottle of very dry sherry somewhere but he did not offer it now. He indicated a chair opposite his own and she sat down.

He began to shuffle the papers before him, extracting those which she needed to sign, and looked up. 'Keeping well?' he said pleasantly. She assured him that she was. 'Good,' he said. 'Now then. If you could just sign here – and again here – where the crosses are.' And he handed her two documents. 'Oh,' he said, 'of course – you'll be needing a pen.' 'It's alright,' she said. 'I've got one.' She opened her handbag and took out a pen and removed the cap. He sat back as if, rather self-consciously, relaxing: determined that she should understand that this episode was all in a day's work. He could hardly not watch her, as she cast an eye over what she was signing her name to before actually writing: it would have been artificial to have looked in any other direction.

Of course she had dressed rather carefully for this occasion. It was a fairly warm day, summer clothes were no longer a sign of naïveté or bumpkin-like over-enthusiasm; she was wearing a very pale linen skirt and a silk jersey. Immaculate, that was the idea. She finished signing and handed the documents back to him. 'Right,' he said. 'And here is your—' but he didn't finish the sentence; there wasn't a way of doing so which wasn't too unspeakably crude: he simply handed her the cheque.

She looked at it: it meant absolutely nothing to her. She had done no calculations; she barely even remembered the amount of the valuation that he'd arranged. He began to explain. 'There's a run-down here of the actual figures,' he said; 'here it is.' 'It's alright,' she said. 'I really don't need to see them.' 'As you like,' he said, replacing the sheet of paper. He closed the folder. The business was done. She put the cheque in her handbag and he looked at his watch. 'I'd offer you lunch,' he said, 'but I'm afraid I'm rather pushed for time – I've got a client due in half an hour.'

She got up. 'Please,' she said, 'I didn't for a moment expect it.' She turned towards the door and he came around the desk to meet her. 'I'll see you out then,' he said, and she followed him down the corridor and through the reception area. The office seemed still to be deserted, everyone except the relief receptionist, who was busy typing and hardly looked up at them, still at lunch. He held open the outer door for her and followed her into the lobby. He was seeing her off the premises good and properly. She pressed the lift button and heard the sound of its ascent from perhaps two floors below.

'Well – ' he said, his face having at last, her departure being imminent, brightened, 'good – lu—' but he never completed the ill-chosen (but none would have been better) word: for, as the lift arrived, in the instant before the doors opened to admit her, she turned around towards him, standing there, relieved, so very, visibly, relieved, and she slapped his face.

The last thing she saw, as the doors of the lift closed between them, was his greyish-blue eyes staring at her, sharp with fright and shock, above the hand (very slightly sunburned, its long fingers splayed) which he had raised to cover the appalling, angry, crimson mark which already burned his fair-skinned cheek. It had made a most discernible sound, that slap. She'd been as gratified as surprised at the sound it had discernibly made. If the relief receptionist had stopped typing she'd very possibly have heard it quite clearly. Nicola hoped most sincerely that the relief receptionist had not in fact stopped typing.

# 65

'You didn't,' said Susannah. 'I mean, you *didn't*. Never! Tell me you're making this up.'

'I can't,' said Nicola. 'Because I'm not. I *did*.'

'My God,' said Susannah. 'If I had some champagne in the house I'd open it now. I've got a good mind to go out and get some.'

'Better not. I mustn't get squiffy, I'm minding Chloe this evening – I should be getting back about now, really; I just thought I'd pop in very quickly on the way. Oh – and furthermore: I had that Scunthorpe interview today.'

'Oh, really? Whereabouts?'

'They borrowed a room at the Arts Council.'

'Was it awful?'

'Yes; horrible. Four of them. Perfectly charming and utterly steely-eyed.'

'So long as you haven't got it.'

'Not the slightest chance. But it's great to have made the shortlist. I might add it to my CV next time. "Shortlisted for position as Assistant to the Director, Scunthorpe Literary Festival." That should jack up my employment profile. Now I'd better get back to little Chloe.'

'I must say they were dashed quick off the mark there.'

'What did you expect?'

Chloe was in the kitchen with her mother eating fish fingers and carrots. 'Oh, there you are,' said a harried-looking Helen. 'Brilliant. Look, you wouldn't mind finishing off her tea, would you? I'd have a chance to bathe and change. She'll just eat this lot, more or less, and then she can have some of this yoghurt and go to bed. Wonderful.' She vanished and Nicola sat down beside the child and began to converse with her. The fish fingers lost their appeal after a while and had to be abandoned – Nicola, eating one, could quite see why – but she ate all the yoghurt. Then Nicola took her upstairs to play for a spell.

'Ah,' said Sam, poking his head around the sitting-room doorway, 'you're both in here, are you? Good. Is she behaving herself? Good. Don't take any nonsense from her, mind. Give her an inch and she'll take an ell. Whatever that is. Won't you?'

Chloe looked up at him in understandable amazement. 'You know what I'm talking about, don't you?' This time she did not say *yeah*, but continued to stare at him wide-eyed, and then she nodded as if in summary dismissal of both the question and its author, and turning crawled away across the floor. 'Still, at least she's got blue eyes,' he said resignedly. 'I suppose that's something.' 'I should say so,' said Nicola, with only a hint of sadness. Ah, but it was. It was certainly something. There was unquestionably something magical about blue eyes.

'Well,' said Sam, 'I'd better get cracking or I'll be in trouble. Again. Excuse me.'

Nicola picked up the baby and sat her on her knee and began to sing to her:

> Mares eat oats
> And does eat oats
> But little lambs eat parsley

while holding her hands and clapping them together on the down beat. Soon the child was enthralled. 'Dozey!' she cried.

'Darzey!' Sam and Helen, coming in to say good-bye and seeing all this, exchanged looks of massive self-congratulation as they left the house. How anyone not the responsible parent could possibly be prevailed upon to look after, let alone play with, an infant child was entirely beyond their comprehension: but never mind that: the freak had come to them, and life had taken on a whole new iridescence.

# 66

Nicola was sitting in a brasserie in Soho with Lizzie drinking vodka and tonics. 'Listen, darling,' said Lizzie, 'Alf saw your friend the other evening. Ran into him in the Middle Temple or somewhere.' 'Oh, good,' said Nicola. 'I'm glad to know he's still around and about.'

'The thing is, why don't you tell me everything that's happened since I last saw you – if you like, that is. I'm not trying to pry.'

'Of course not.'

'I ought to have been in touch much sooner but you know how it is.'

'Of course I do.'

'Henrietta's had chicken pox.'

'Oh dear. Poor Henrietta.'

'She got it from Fergus.'

'Oh dear.'

'At Easter.'

'What a drag.'

'Children are funny that way.'

'Poor little things.'

'Have you been alright then?'

'Mostly.' She began to give Lizzie a résumé of the events of the past several weeks, ending up with the Scunthorpe interview. 'But that's extraordinary,' exclaimed Lizzie. 'I'm producing a programme about the Scunthorpe Festival for Channel Four. How marvellous to have you on the spot.'

'But I won't be.'

'You might be.'

'Hardly.'

'We'll see. Perhaps I'll have a word with—'

'Don't you dare!'

'Alright. Whatever you say.'

'Not that I'm ungrateful, but—'

'No, you're right of course. Still it might be rather interesting, as these things go.'

'Yes, I'm almost sorry I won't be involved. I only applied on a sort of bloody-minded whim. Just after Jonathan sacked me, you see. I was feeling rather mental.'

'Poor Nicola. Was it really that bad, then?'

'Yes.'

'Then perhaps I can offer some consolation.'

'How's that?'

'As I mentioned, an eminent member of the junior bar, not noted for any tendency to embroider or otherwise obscure the truth, has reported your friend—'

'Ex-friend.'

' – your ex-friend, sighted earlier this week in the environs of the Middle Temple – I *think* it was the Middle Temple – where was I up to?'

'The subordinate clause following your, that is, *my*, ex-friend.'

'Oh, yes. Well, the ex-friend gave the impression – so I'm *told* – that life had lost all its sweetness. He appeared to be both careworn and melancholy, in a tight-lipped sort of way. My silks and fine array/My smiles and languished air/By love are driven away/And mournful lean despair/Comes with yew to deck my grave/Such end true lovers have, sort of aspect.'

'Gosh. Are you *quite* sure?'

'That was pretty much the look of it.'

'What bloody cheek.'

'Still, better miserable now, and through his own fault, and therefore deservedly so, than not at all.'

'Poor Jonathan.'

'You don't still—'

'No. No no no no no!'

# 67

'Susannah, something awful has happened.'

'Then why are you grinning like that?'

'Because it's so funny.'

'Oh, I see. You've got the Scunthorpe job. Nicola, how *could* you?'

'It's not *my* fault. It's not as if I'd *tried*.'

'So it *is* your fault. If only you'd tried you wouldn't have got it. Oh, well, no harm done, you can just turn it down. You *are* going to turn it down, aren't you?'

'No, I'm not. I can't. I haven't. They rang me at work today, you see. The daytime telephone number. And I accepted.'

'Oh, how *could* you? Why?'

'Well, what else could I do? I mean, it would have looked so bad. It's absolutely out of the question, to back off at this stage. At least without a very good reason. I was on the spot, I really had to accept.'

'Oh, *hell*.'

'No, it's good, really. Six months in Scunthorpe, why not?'

'Oh, Nicola, I can't *believe* this. But anyway—you won't be up there all the time, will you?'

'Well, I might be doing a bit of popping up and down, I suppose.'

'When do you start?'

'On the first of June. Just a month from now. I've already given in my notice.'

'That's that then. How *awful*.'

'No it isn't. It'll be very good for my career. I'll be getting some publicity experience, and all sorts. They wanted an all-rounder, you see; someone flexible, not too set in their ways.'

'So they chose you.'

'Yes. They must have seen me on the dance floor at one of those clubs.'

'Probably. They have spies everywhere.'

'Yes: arts administration and allied trades is the big game in town, after all.'

'Soon they'll be nudging each other as you pass them on your way to a good table at *le restaurant du bon ton* and muttering, don't look now, but that's Nicola Gatling.'

'They could even be doing it already. Or would be, if I were actually on my way to a good table, or any table, at *le restaurant du bon ton*. Oh, but that reminds me: can you all come out to dinner next Saturday night, on me? There's an amusing new place I've heard about on this side of the *fleuve*, and I thought I'd ask you all and Philip and Jean-Claude. Time for a tiny little party. What do you say?'

'I say wonderful idea. Thank you, Nicola.'

'You see there's just one more chore I have to do. This will be a reward for reaching the end of the whole routine. I dare say you know the routine to which I allude.'

'Guess I do, honey. Ruby Keeler never worked harder.'

'So I'll book a table for tomorrow week.'

'Whizzy.'

'What's whizzy?'

'Oh, there you are. Nicola's taking us out to dine in an amusing new restaurant next Saturday night.'

'Me too?'

'Yes, you too!'

'Wow, that's *whizzy*. Shall I go and tell Dad?'

'You do that.' Guy ran off, and came back a minute later.

'Did you tell him?'
'Yes.'
'What did he say?'
'He said, whizzy.'
'Truly?'
'Yes, truly, he did. Whizzy, he said.'
'That's whizzy.'

# 68

She'd forgotten entirely to give Jonathan her keys: but that turned out to be rather a good thing than not, in the circumstances.

> Dear Jonathan,
>    I'm sorry this has taken so long to organise – but I thought of collecting the rest of my things next Saturday at around 2 p.m. if that suits you. I still – sorry for the oversight – have the keys, so I could let myself in in your absence and then lock up and leave the keys for you in an envelope in the letter box downstairs. Please let me know if this arrangement is in any way inconvenient.
>
> Yours,<br>Nicola

Receiving no reply to this letter Nicola assumed very reasonably that the arrangement was in fact a convenient one; at the appointed time she was to be seen letting herself into the building.

She had rigorously banished all thought of the distress she might suffer in coming here once more – and then in leaving, once more, and finally: oh, how she had cautioned and lectured herself! She ran up all the stairs as quickly as she could as if to show herself how paltry an undertaking this truly was. A woman dressed in pink jeans couldn't be supposed to be engaged upon anything grave or momentous, anything which could stop the heart. She arrived at the second floor, at the door which had for so long been her very own; she unlocked it, and taking a deep breath, entered the flat.

The silence was appalling. Her presence seemed to violate some secret force which was now in possession of the place; she almost expected hands to reach out from the walls and seize hold of her so as to inhibit her progress. In the hope of eluding them she passed as quickly as she could down the short passageway leading from the front door so as to enter the large bright space of the sitting room: there, surely, she would find some ghostly welcome – or if not a welcome, some ghostly acknowledgement, at least, of her right to be here on this one, last, occasion. She had glimpsed already the brilliant, almost-white glare of the sunshine pouring into the room: now she entered it.

The shock of its dazzling brightness passed in a stunning instant, to be replaced by a new and yet deeper impression of silence. Here, in the sunlit emptiness, the silence was more terrible still. She sat down, trembling, on the edge of the sofa, marvelling, almost stricken. I should not have come here, she thought. I can't manage it after all. I am not as brave as I thought.

But I am here, she told herself sternly: I must simply get on with what I have to do. So that was what she did, rising from her seat, and almost blindly, forcing herself, retracing her steps, and going into the bedroom to open the wardrobe where she supposed her remaining possessions still to be as she had left them so many weeks ago.

But here a further shock awaited her. For if the silence of the flat had appalled and even frightened her before, it now seemed to assault her. It told her that she had no right to be here, none: this silence seemed to emanate from a force darker and more secret still than that which possessed the sitting room and passageway. This room was forbidden not only to her but to all sentient creatures. This room, with its mahogany wardrobe, its discreetly magnificent bed, its north-facing windows through which she could – even now – see the tops of the trees in the communal gardens swaying in the breeze of a spring afternoon, was a habitation now only for denial, desolation and grief: for whatever dark spirits are sucked into the vacuum left by the departure of tenderness, love and trust. She perceived this in an instant, clearly: Jonathan had evidently perceived it too: she could see that he had not returned to this room either. It had been abandoned altogether. Denial, desolation and grief stroked her with their frail detaining fingers and whispered to her in their tiny keening voices; she crossed the room and turning the large iron key which secured them opened the doors of the wardrobe.

There were her boxes, just as she had left them; hanging from the brass rail above them, nothing. Nothing, nothing but black and empty space: not so much as a coat hanger remained in the belly of this great wardrobe which she had so admired. Here, it uncannily seemed, was the heart of the calamity which filled this room and beyond it the entire flat – here, and not – as might crudely have been assumed – the bed, which stood expressionless, passionless, neutral, in its place. No: here, in the darkness of the empty wardrobe, was the correlative of all their anguish. She took the boxes into the corridor one by one and left them near the front door, and then having cast one final glance from the threshold at the bereaved room, she quietly closed the door.

She was mourning now, and knew it. The death was fully and finally acknowledged, the obsequies could begin. And what could she do, what should be done, in the way of a funeral rite for a creature so frail, so incorporeal, as the life she and Jonathan had shared? She should at least pay it a minute or two of candid and final farewell; she should at any rate sit once more on that sofa (they'd paid an arm and a leg for it, and joyfully) in the dazzling silence of that midsummer-sky-blue room. That much at least she should do. Nicola entered the room once more, and once more sat down on the edge of the sofa, and submitted to the stream of memories, impressions, reflections which began now to unwind like a film on the screen of her grieving consciousness.

# 69

'Oh — I'm sorry! I—'

'No, *I'm* sorry — I thought you'd be gone by now, I would've—'

'No, well, yes, I should've been, I was delayed — I'll just—'

'Look—' he hovered in the doorway, as helpless as she: each as dreadful to the other as an apparition: now he took a few uncertain steps into the room. 'As you're here,' he said, 'as we've met like this — there was something I wanted to say to you.'

She was speechless; she trembled. 'I would've written,' he said, 'but — anyway — look — could we sit down for a moment?'

And still trembling, still speechless, she sat down. He came hesitantly across the room and sat carefully down on the other end of the sofa. He made a helpless gesture. 'I just wanted,' he said, 'to say that I'm sorry.'

'Sorry,' she repeated stupidly. 'What do you mean?'

'I'm sorry for — everything. For what's happened.'

'Oh.'

'Do you understand?'

'No. No, I don't. I don't know what you mean.'

'I've made a mistake. I've made a *terrible*, an absolutely terrible mistake.'

'Oh, I see.'

'I was wrong.'

She couldn't truly take this in. It was difficult for him to go on speaking, but she couldn't help him. 'I don't understand how it happened,' he went on. 'I don't actually truly understand *what's* happened. It's just – it was just wrong. *I* was wrong.'

'You're saying—'

'I shouldn't have sent you away. I shouldn't have said that I didn't love you. I've – I've just – screwed up. I mean – look – I'm just—' and he started to cry. He sat there, crying: it was a dreadful sight: but she could do nothing.

'Jonathan, don't,' she said; 'don't, don't.' 'No,' he said, his tears ceasing. 'It's hardly reasonable, is it, after everything I've done.' There was an awful silence, black as night: they felt as if they were staring into the depths of an abyss. The silence itself seemed to echo, in that awful blackness. It was he who eventually spoke. 'Can you forgive me?' he said.

'I don't know. I can't say.' It was too much to take in, in truth. 'Please,' he said wretchedly, 'please – you must forgive me. I mean, you see – you see, if you can't, if you don't, then my life really won't be worth living.' He was looking at her, his blue eyes not cold any longer but blazing: he was altogether serious; he truly believed that his life would not be worth living. 'It's too much to ask,' she said, 'that the worth of your life should depend on me, on an act of mine.'

'Yes,' he said. 'One always asks too much.'

But she dimly saw that it might be her life which would not be worth living were she not to forgive him. 'I'll do the best I can,' she said. There was another silence; he was struggling for speech. 'I – ' he began, 'I hope – I was wondering if there was anything, anything whatever, I can do for you, now, or ever – you see, now, I – look – can I see you again? Will you let me see you again?'

'I don't know. I'm going away soon, anyway.'

'*What?*'

She told him about Scunthorpe. He was devastated; he sat there, helpless, defeated. Then his spirits seemed just fractionally to rally. 'You must take the car,' he said. 'You'll need one, up there.' Here was something he could do for her, immediately.

'No, I couldn't possibly.' And it was quite a classy Renault. 'Yes, you could; you must. It's the least I can do. You can take it now if you like.' She explained that she had Susannah's car. 'I've probably got a parking ticket by now,' she said. 'I really must go.' But she sat there, helpless, disoriented. He looked out of the window. The sun still streamed into the room where they sat, amazed and fearful: while all the ghosts waited in the walls. He took her hand. 'Could you just let me hope, for the moment,' he said; 'just let me believe, for the moment, that I can somehow repair everything? That I can – somehow – eventually – make it all right? Can you let me hope for that? At least for the moment?' She said nothing: what could she truly say? She looked at him. Who was this stranger? 'I love you, Nicola,' he said. He saw the look in her eyes, and let go of her hand. 'No – yes – of course you can't possibly believe this now, I do see that—'

'Can you?'

Could anyone, at any time? 'We'll see,' he said. 'I'll show you. I'll devote myself to showing you; *I'll find a way.*' She fought down an impulse to say, don't, please don't. Suddenly she felt entirely depleted, as if at any moment she might herself begin to cry: and why should this be so? Then she remembered the keys; she took them from her handbag and gave them to him. He hesitated slightly before taking them from her. Then a thought seemed to strike him. 'By the way,' he said, 'do you like rubies?'

'*Rubies?*'

'Yes, that's right, rubies.'

'I've never thought.'

'I just wondered.'

'I see.'

Perhaps he was mad. Anything, she now knew, was possible. 'Look, I really must go now,' she told him. 'Susannah will be wanting the car.' Jonathan made a shrug of resignation. 'Give me your telephone number, will you?' he said. She wrote it down for him, and then he helped her downstairs with the boxes.

He leaned on the window frame and looked at her anxiously 'Drive carefully,' he told her. 'Of course.' 'I'll call you – oh! look, I almost forgot – you left that marmalade—'

'That what?'

'The marmalade my mother sent you, I'll just—'

'For God's sake.' She began to laugh. He looked bewildered; he tried to smile. 'You eat it,' she said.

'Are you sure?'

'Yes, I'm absolutely certain.'

'Oh, thanks, thanks, I will then.'

'Bon appétit!'

She let in the clutch. She could hardly bear to look at his face, just at this moment: it harrowed her. Then she waved briefly and drove away.

When she reached Chelsea, she did not cross the river immediately, but parked near the Embankment, and went and hung over the wall, staring for a long time down at the water while the traffic roared dreadfully past her back, and wondering why she could not – just now – feel anything other than an all-engulfing, and quite unutterable, sadness.

GAYLORD F